Recaptured Heart

Priscilla T. Poole Rainwater

PublishAmerica
Baltimore

First printing

All characters appearing in this work are fictitious. Any resemblance to real persons, living or dead, is purely coincidental.

ISBN: 1-4241-0386-X
PUBLISHED BY PUBLISHAMERICA, LLLP
www.publishamerica.com
Baltimore

Printed in the United States of America

Prologue

The principal of Thurman R. Cline High School stood at the podium. "Family and friends, I give you the graduating class of 1981. I wish them all the luck."

Bright young men and women with so much hope and promise stood, tossed their graduation caps in the air and cheered loudly.

Jackie Williams, the class valedictorian, ran to her father, smiling, and then hugged him. Nearby, a friend of the family snapped a photo of the two of them, then wished them well.

Looking up at her father, she studied him with genuine concern. His usual rich ebony complexion had a gray tint. "Are you okay, Daddy?"

She gently wiped drops of moisture from his damp forehead. Privately, Jackie hoped and prayed she could get through college and get a good paying job somewhere. She wanted to take care of her father, he deserved to have a comfortable life.

If all went as she planned, he could retire in four years. She had been working at a furniture store who's owner was the father of a close friend of hers. She had managed to save quite a bit of money. That, along with her full scholarship, would alleviate any extra financial strain her father would have otherwise had to bear.

Covering his daughter's hands with his own, Evart Williams exchanged a smile with her, then shook his head. Pride and joy washed over him. *She's brought me nothing but happiness,* he thought to himself. She looked so much like her mother. The same cocoa brown skin, long wavy black hair, exotic oval face, and intense whisky colored eyes. Evan was ashamed to admit, even to himself, that it sometimes hurt to look at Jackie, her being the mirror image of the woman he had loved and lost.

"I'm fine, pumpkin." He gave her a reassuring hug.

Suddenly, he frowned as he spotted Jackie's friend, Chad, making his way towards them. Jackie and Chad had been friends since the seventh grade, a friendship he had never been comfortable with. Evart knew Chad was a good boy. He came from a well-to-do family in the community, and his parents were good people who liked Jackie. Chad himself was the All American type. Tall, blond, blue eyed, and athletic. Evart supposed Chad was what was considered a good catch for some lucky young lady, but not for his little girl, no sir.

He had seen the look in Chad's eyes when he was around Jackie, they were filled with love, the same look of love he had had for Jackie's mother. It didn't help the situation at all that Jackie was also in love with Chad.

As far as Evart was concerned, it wasn't an issue of race, or Chad hurting his little girl, he trusted Chad. The issue was that they lived in a small mountain town, and such relationships were not exactly embraced openly or warmly. His worst fear was his girl (or even Chad) being hurt by anyone else. Because of that fear, he had had a long talk with Jackie about their friendship. She had promised she would keep her feelings in check.

Evart was relieved when Jackie decided to go to college for the summer instead of waiting for the fall session. He hoped that in time their feelings would abate, what with the time apart and everything. Feelings he could see both had been fighting hard not to act on.

Jackie turned to see who her father was giving such a hard look at, and smiled when she saw who it was.

"Jackie, we did it! I was so proud of you giving your speech," Chad said excitedly.

He swept her up in his arms, gave her a big smile, then buried his face in her thick hair. He then set her down gently, and pushed a wayward strand of hair off her pretty face.

She took a deep unsteady breath and stepped back. She knew he would be gone for three months, along with his good friend and fellow classmate Robert. They would be backpacking across Europe with a tour group. Chad's parents had given him the trip as a graduation gift. He had asked her to come along, but she refused, not only because of her promise to her father, but she wanted to start college as soon as possible.

Chad interrupted her thoughts. "Mom and Dad want you to have this."

He handed her an envelope, which she accepted with a sad smile. She was really wishing she could feel so care free and join him on his trip. But, she had her promises to keep, both to herself, and her dad.

"Thank your parents for me, Chad, and have a great time. Write me when you can."

"Sure. Look, Mom and Dad are waiting for me in the car. I

have to be at the airport in a few hours. Bye, love."

Jackie spied some of his other friends coming over, the same friends who had never approved of or liked her and Chad's friendship. She decided to leave. Hugging him one last time, she backed away.

"I better get going. Kathy's folks are throwing us a graduation party. I'll miss you, Chad."

Turning, she took her father's hand and walked away.

Chad watched as she strolled away, nodding at a few people as she moved through the crowd. He would miss her, too, and he also vowed to himself that when he returned home from his trip he would tell her that he was in love with her. *Just please don't let her laugh in my face,* Chad thought.

She had never shown any interest beyond them being just friends, and he wondered how he would ever get her to give him a chance to be more. But he planned on doing just that.

"Chad, are you going to give me a goodbye kiss?"

He swung his head around to see Misty standing behind him. He frowned, as she slowly unzipped her graduation gown to show off the tight, skimpy designer dress. Her blue eyes narrowed.

"I'm surprised you're not with that...that...Jackie," she said, giving him a hard look.

Completely irritated, Chad turned and left. *I don't have to explain myself, or my feelings about Jackie, to anyone,* he thought.

Misty flushed, and tried her best to hide her embarrassment in front of her friends.

Chapter 1

Jackie sat looking at the reunion invitation. "I can't believe it's been ten years," she mumbled to herself as she looked around the office. In six years she had climbed to the top at the advertising agency. She had worked hard, but still, there was something missing in her life. Maybe getting back to her hometown would help her get a handle on things. She would probably see Chad, and she found the thought very satisfying. Closing her eyes, she went back in time. *We really were different as night and day.* She chuckled. He was the captain of the football team, and she was the shy black girl who was the class brain, a real bookworm. Every high school has a social structure, and it was amazing, still, that she and Chad had actually been friends.

The friendship began in the seventh grade. One afternoon some boys from the junior varsity team wanted to pick on some helpless nerd, and that day, she was the target.

Classes had been dismissed early. She had been getting her books together when four huge boys came around the corner. The biggest of the four spoke up. "Look guys, Jackie needs help."

Well, their idea of "help" was knocking her books out of her hands, then shoving her back and forth between them.

Suddenly a stern, intimidating voice barked, "Cut it out!" There stood Chad, glaring at the bullies.

They weren't used to being challenged by anyone, least of all, by one of their "own", a popular jock. They figured a couple of half-hearted snide remarks were enough to save face, then they left.

Chad helped her with her books, then offered to walk her home. From that day on, a close friendship developed between them. She learned that he wasn't just another dumb jock. He was nearly as smart as she was! While she wasn't a conceited girl in any sense, she *knew* she was intelligent.

They spent time talking about her plans of going to university three states away, and his plans of going to community college to get a business degree, then help run his family's four furniture stores.

He could have went to almost any college of his choice, but his father was not in good health, and he felt it was important for him to be there to help out in any way he could. While most high school kids his age spent the weekend partying and drinking, Chad would spend time with her, watching cheesy horror movies, studying, and doing homework. His parents mentioned on several occasions that she was a positive influence on Chad. Jackie also remembered that there were others who didn't approve of their friendship.

They didn't like the fact that one of "their own" spent time with the class "nerd." After all, she didn't come from a well-to-do family, and she was black, in a predominantly white small town. She had told Chad on several occasions that she didn't think they should hang out so much. That his friends had made it quite clear they didn't want her around.

"Jackie, I don't care what they think. As long as we're friends, that's all that matters to me," was his usual retort. And he would usually say this as he was gazing into her eyes lovingly, occasionally running his fingers through her thick black hair. He seemed to love touching her hair, he even got very upset when she talked about cutting it.

"Jackie, promise me that you won't cut it off. I love your hair."

She would always give him his promise.

Snapping back to the present, she thought, *Chad, I kept my promise.*

Twisting a lock of her hair, she found herself wondering if he still looked the same. Did he still have the same toned body? She could remember everything about him, from his corn silk blond hair, to his blue eyes, shining with so much promise. She hadn't forgotten a single detail. Would he even remember her? Hopefully, but people change. Maybe they had both changed so much that the flame that burned before wouldn't even be a dying ember this many years later, much less spark again.

She knew *she* had changed, after her father's sudden death, not long after high school graduation. She had left, and never returned to her hometown. She became driven by a single minded obsession to make a success of herself, and nothing else mattered at the time.

She graduated college with honors, and went on to become one of the youngest executives in her firm. Even her body had transformed. From awkward young girl, to a sensual woman who had her fair share of male admirers.

Picking up the phone, she dialed her friend and fellow "nerd", Kathy Henderson.

Kathy was always spunky, and full of life. Jackie loved spending time with her, she was always a lot of fun to be around.

"Hi, Kathy, I got the reunion invitation. I was wondering if you could pick me up at the airport. That is, if I can make it."

She knew she was kidding herself. She would make it, and *wanted* to make it there as well.

Kathy let out a delighted giggle. "Neat! I'm looking forward to it! It will be just like old times. I can't wait to see Chad's face when he sees you. By the way, did you know that Misty Tate is *still* after him?"

Jackie gripped the phone, remembering Misty very well. Pretty, blond, prom queen, cheerleader, bitch from hell. She had taken great pleasure in telling Jackie how Chad had spent the night with her after the prom.

Hearing that had hurt Jackie, though she tried her best not to let it show. And despite the fact that she had went to the prom with another fellow, Samuel Richardson. But Chad had spent most of his time dancing with and hanging out with Jackie. Well, at least he was when Misty wasn't hanging all over him.

Of course, the highlight of the night for Misty was when she and Chad were crowned prom king and queen.

Kathy's laugh snapped her back to the present once again.

"You can stay with me. All the old bunch will be coming, too. I'm so excited!

The entire "old bunch" were, of course, the nerds and outcasts that all stuck together in order to make high school more bearable.

"Okay, you talked me into it, I'll come. You know, it will be good to see you all of you again."

Kathy laughed. "You mean to see Chad, right? He has to be one of the best looking white men I know."

Jackie couldn't help but laugh. "Yeah, I *do* want to see him. We lost contact over the years. He's probably married and had a house full of kids by now."

Kathy giggled like a little girl with a secret, and what she said both startled and pleased Jackie.

"He's not even in a serious relationship. I know. I interviewed him last week for our newspaper. Jackie, he asked about you. He wanted to know if you were married, or had children, or any of the above. Maybe you two could get together, times *have* changed you know."

Jackie leaned back in her chair thinking. *So, he asked about me. But it's probably because we were such close friends for so long. And with the reunion so close and all, he was probably just curious, that's all.*

"Listen, Kathy, I need to go and ask the boss for some time off. So I'll see you in two days, alright?"

After saying her goodbyes, Jackie made arrangements to leave for the reunion.

Her boss was more than happy to accommodate her. In her six years with the company she had never taken vacation time, and her hard work had brought some big money into the company. He wanted to keep her happy and productive.

***

"Chad, you *have* to go to the reunion. Besides, don't you want to see how some of our classmates turned out?" Robert asked, looking at his best friend.

"I don't want to spend the weekend playing remember-when with a bunch of people I never liked. And I sure don't want to spend the whole evening dodging Misty," Chad replied.

13

Robert laughed as he headed for his Mustang. "Yeah, she is something. But you know I saw Kathy yesterday, and she said Jackie will be coming. *you two* were friends, remember? Don't you want to see her?"

Hearing Jackie's name, Chad's heart went pitter-patter.

"Yeah, well, I thought we were friends, but she never came back; never answered any of my letters or returned any of my calls. She made it pretty clear she didn't want to be bothered with me." A swift shadow of pain swept across Chad's face.

Robert knew how Chad felt about Jackie. He just couldn't understand how his friend could hold a torch for so long, for one woman. But Chad was his friend, and he would support him no matter what.

"Man, I saw how you were around her, and why you two never got together is beyond me. And please don't give me that crap about you're white and she's black. Listen, this may your last chance. Ever. You've been pining away for ten long years man!"

Chad ran his hands over his face. He knew Robert was right. Even if she didn't have any feelings for him, he at least wanted to see her again. He wondered if she had changed much. Smiling, he thought about her long wavy hair, and her sunny smile. Her whisky colored eyes, so intense. Hell, he had loved everything about her. But what he had loved the most was how she had made him feel.

"Alright, I'll go," Chad said.

"Great! Let's go grab something to eat. I need to build up my strength. I have a date with a hot little waitress from the club."

Chad shook his head. Robert had more women in his life than Hugh Hefner.

As he climbed into his car he wondered why he had never told Jackie how he felt about her. Deep inside he knew it had to

14

do with race, afraid that she would reject him because he was white.

When Kathy had interviewed him for the business section of the town newspaper, she had told him that Jackie was a big success, working for an advertising agency. And that she was still single. And not dating anyone.

Maybe I can still win her heart, Chad thought as he pulled out of the parking lot.

Chapter 2

"Girl, you look great! I swear, if that dress doesn't get Mr. Tall, Blond and Handsome, nothing will!"

Smoothing her strapless lilac dress, Jackie smiled. "Oh? And what makes you think I wore this to impress him?" she asked, taking one final look at the back of her dress, pleased with how it clung to her figure.

Kathy rolled her eyes. "Oh please. You spent over an hour primping in that mirror, fussing with all that hair. You need to get that mess cut short, that way you can wash-and-go."

Jackie hated to admit that she had spent that amount of time fussing in the mirror, but there it was. And she knew why, even if she wouldn't admit it to herself.

"Well, I promised someone a long time ago that I would never cut it," she said with a mysterious little smile, a smile that she herself was unaware of.

They both stood in the doorway of their old high school gymnasium, giving each other the once-over before going in.

***

Jackie smiled as she stepped inside the gym, thinking about old times. They made their way to the table that had been reserved for them. Of course it was the table with the nerds, bookworms, computer geeks and other over achievers. And Jackie loved seeing them all.

For the next hour everyone shared their life experiences, talked shop, and shared trade secrets.

"Well, would you look at this. Some things never change."

Jackie didn't have to look to know who the whiny, nasal voice belonged to. And sure enough, there stood Misty Tate and her sneering pack of friends.

"Misty, you're looking…uhmm…well," Jackie said, taking a drink of her club soda to wash the nasty taste out of her mouth.

She's right, some things never change, especially people like her, Jackie thought.

Despite herself, Jackie felt slightly threatened. Misty was still blonde and pretty as ever, and in a dress that was a size too small. She had kept herself in shape over the years.

Okay, maybe I'm being a little bitchy and paranoid, Jackie thought.

But deep down she knew better. In high school Misty had always went out of her way to make Jackie's life miserable.

"You know, Chad tells me I look *great* every time he sees me," Misty said with an innocent, yet vicious little smile.

Misty's friends cackled dutifully, and the sound of it made Jackie's skin crawl.

"Well, well, there he is now. Chad! Oh, Chaaad!" Misty sang as she charged towards him. Her friends snickered and followed suit.

Kathy leaned over to Jackie, grinning.

"Look at that cow! No pride at all!"

Kathy shifted gears.

"But goodness girl, get a load of him," she whispered, unable to hide the excitement in her voice. Excitement at the prospect of Jackie and Chad meeting once again, and the possible outcome.

Jackie could hardly breathe. He looked simply amazing. The blue suit he was wearing accentuated his deep dark tan, and fit his tall body well.

He was chatting with some people Jackie didn't recognize, and of course, Misty.

Jackie decided to get herself together.

Grabbing her evening bag, she made a dash to the ladies room.

***

Looking at herself in the mirror, Jackie wondered if she had made the wrong choice in coming.

Maybe I should have left the past, and the love of a young naïve girl, well enough alone, Jackie thought.

"Hey, aren't you Jackie Williams?"

Jackie glanced over at the woman who had recognized her.

Great, another one of Misty's cronies. The woman must have called in the Bitch Patrol to come after me Jackie thought, and merely nodded at her.

"I'm Linda Owens. Remember me?" She put a tentative hand on Jackie's shoulder. "You look great! I hear you're a big success in media or something, right?

I can't believe she's actually being nice to me. She used to be one of Misty's biggest hangers-on, Jackie thought.

18

"Uhmm, yes. I work in advertising."

Linda crossed her arms and gave Jackie a serious, meaningful look.

"You know, I'm glad you came. I wanted to tell you how sorry I was for the mean way we treated you, when we were in school."

Trying her best not to show her shock and dismay, Jackie replied, "Well, thank you, that was very thoughtful of you to say. We *were* only kids, and it was a long time ago, but the fact that you still remember tells me you're sincere."

Linda flashed her a big smile, nodded, turned to leave, and stopped once more.

"You know, Misty always was jealous of you."

Saying that, she turned and finally left.

"Misty jealous of *me?* Yeah, right" Jackie mumbled and half-chuckled.

Frowning into the mirror, she thought of Misty. The blond goddess who strolled through life batting her pretty blue eyes, and always getting whoever or whatever she wanted. And from what she had heard so far, she was still doing it.

Double checking herself in the mirror, she reapplied her lip gloss, took a deep breath, and turned to go back to the gym.

***

As she walked back to her table, Robert Buckland headed towards her. He had always reminded her of a rugged Billy Zane, only taller and more muscular. He stopped in front of her, so close that she had to lean back to keep his lips from touching her face. Undeterred, he grabbed her, pulled her close in a hug, and gave her a peck on the cheek. Then he stepped back, took her hands, and looked her up and down.

"Jackie, sweetheart, time has been very kind to you," he said with a smile.

"Thanks, Robert. You look great." She felt a bit embarrassed by Robert's open appraisal of her body.

Jackie glanced around and spotted Misty sitting at her table with her friends, all of them glaring in her direction.

"Well, Chad's here somewhere. C'mon, sweetheart, let's go find him."

She had no time to protest as he draped his arms over her shoulders and guided her towards a group of men standing at the far side of the gym.

She recognized all of them as former football players. Chad was among them, talking and laughing about their high school days.

Robert leaned down and whispered, "You know, he wasn't going to come until I told him that you would be here."

Jackie stopped and looked at him, stunned, not believing what she had just heard. He gave her a wicked grin and another peck on the cheek. Chad froze the minute he saw Jackie, his blue eyes piercing her. He strode forward and stopped in front of her, his knees knocking. He pulled her from Robert's grasp and wrapped his strong arms around her in a fierce embrace. He was so overjoyed he felt like crying. Oh, to hold her again! How could he ever have let her go, the woman he'd never stopped loving?

Neither one of them noticed that practically every eye in the place was on them. Robert and Kathy stood side by side, beaming.

Chad smiled as a familiar song from their school days began playing; "Waiting for a Girl Like You," by Foreigner.

He took her hand and lead her towards the dance floor. Gathering her into his arms, he held her firmly, yet gently.

Only as they began swaying to the music did he speak. "God, Jackie, you look wonderful."

She closed her eyes, enjoying his closeness and warmth. She could have sworn her heart was beating in tune with the music. She sighed. "You look great, Chad. I heard from Kathy that your business is doing very well."

He smiled and shrugged dismissively. "Yeah, business is good, but that's not what I wanted to talk to you about. I want to know why you didn't come back?" He couldn't hide the pain in his voice, and didn't particularly care to.

She tried to step back away from him, but he tensed and wouldn't let her escape his grasp. "Chad, after Dad died there was nothing left for me here."

Hearing those words made his heart sink. "Jackie, nothing left here for you? What about me? I was here."

That was all Chad got out as suddenly Misty materialized out of nowhere, pulling at his arm and doing her best to dislodge Jackie from his embrace. "Chad darling, they want us for a group picture. You know, all you friends from the old gang," Misty said as she shot a nasty look at Jackie.

The last thing Chad wanted was to let Jackie go.

Not wanting a confrontation, Jackie said, "Go ahead. Maybe we can talk later."

Jackie hoped her disappointment didn't show too much.

"Come on Chad, they're waiting on us," Misty whined. Her whining really grated on his nerves. It always had.

He was trying to pull his arm free of her death grip, but before he succeeded Jackie turned and walked off. Chad snapped "Let go of me! I've got to take care of something important!" He snatched his arm free.

I've don't have the time or patience for her silly-ass games Chad thought. *I've got to tell Jackie how I feel about her. Oh please, please let her feel the same way.*

21

***

Kathy was talking so fast that Jackie didn't have time to answer.

"Honey, you two were made for one another. If you two had been dancing any closer you would have been doing the nasty right there in front of everyone. What did he say anyway?"

"Look, Kat, would you mind if we go now? I need some time to think." *Chad asked me why I didn't come back to him. How can I answer that when I'm not even sure myself* Jackie thought.

Kathy looked disappointed.

"Do you really want to go? I mean, you should wait and talk to Chad. At least say good night to him,"

Jackie wanted to stay, then turned, only to see Misty hanging off Chad like a cheap suit. Somehow she had cajoled Chad into returning to have some reunion photos taken. She was really mugging it up for the camera too, smiling as if she'd won the lottery.

Jackie wanted to go before she professed her true feelings, and perhaps making a fool of herself in the process. After all, maybe he just wanted to have his old friend back, nothing more And there was *no way* she was going to risk looking the fool in front of Misty of all people.

Turning to Kathy she said "No, I want to go. He's pretty busy anyway, he won't miss me."

Kathy grabbed her purse and wrap. "Okay, but I'll meet you at the car, I need to go to the ladies room."

Jackie made her way out of the building, smiling and waving goodbye to several people. When she found Kathy's car she leaned against it, enjoying the clear mountain air and sound of nocturnal insects. She closed her eyes and smiled, thinking about how wonderful it felt being in Chad's arms, him holding her so close. Just the feel of his hands on her body aroused her. "Jackie, were you going to just leave again without saying goodbye?" The sound of Chad's voice snapped her out of her day dream. He was standing right in front of her. *My God in heaven. Was I that preoccupied with him that I didn't even hear him walk right up to me?* Jackie thought.

Jackie stammered, "I figured you would be busy with Misty and...your friends," then turned her face away from him.

He touched her cheek in a wistful gesture, and gently turned her face so he could look into her eyes. When he spoke, his voice raised slightly in irritation.

"Jackie, I want us to talk, You could have waited for me you know."

He blew out a long breath, and tried to keep his emotions in check. Then he pulled her close, and she dropped her chin on his chest with a sigh of pleasure.

"What is there to talk about Chad?"

He let out an audible growl of frustration and anger. "We have a lot to talk about, Jackie. For one, Mom wants to see you. Why don't I come get you in the morning so we can go see her together."

Not waiting for a reply, he continued. "Everyone is going to the old Potter swimming hole. We can go and spend afternoon, just like old times. What do you say?"

As he pulled her closer she put her hands on his chest, feeling the hard muscles beneath her fingertips.

"Alright, what time do you want me to be ready?"

She couldn't help herself, he was successfully disarming all her common sense with his touch.

"How about eight in the morning? We'll have breakfast with Mom."

She nodded and smiled.

She saw Kathy and Robert making their way over, so they said their good nights and went their separate ways. Chad and Robert stood watching Kathy's car pull away.

"So, did you tell her how you feel?" Robert asked.

Chad shook his head, kicking a small pebble at his feet. Robert gave his friend a dumbfounded look.

"Damn, what are you waiting for."

Chad shrugged, and began fiddling with his car keys. "I didn't think it was the right time."

He was still trying to keep himself in check. When Kathy told him Jackie was leaving, all he wanted to do was go to her. He simply couldn't let her leave again without telling her what he should have told her ten years ago. He wanted her so much his body ached.

"She's coming to see Mom with me in the morning, and going swimming with us, too." *I'll tell her tomorrow exactly how I feel, and hope for the best* he thought to himself.

"Look, Rob, I'll see you tomorrow. I've had about all I can take of Misty, I'm gonna head home."

Robert chuckled as he watched him leave.

***

No matter what Jackie did, she couldn't get to sleep. The night just seemed to drag on and on. Finally, seven in the morning rolled around. She jumped out of bed and showered. After changing outfits twice, she decided on a peasant blouse, jeans, and sandals. Fixing her hair up in a single braid, she hurried and wrapped her brown two piece string bikini in a beach towel.

She tiptoed out of the house, knowing that Kathy was still asleep. She went out on the porch to wait for Chad, and sat down on the steps. As she sat waiting, she spotted two rabbits hopping across the yard.

She suddenly realized how much she missed the small town. For ten years she had worked hard to push her life behind her, not wanting to admit, even to herself, that she could have been happy if she had stayed.

The sound of an engine roused her from her thoughts. It was Chad's car, he pulled up a short time later, waving and smiling. Getting up from the steps, she grabbed her towel.

"Good morning." She smiled. His mere presence gave her such great joy.

"Good morning, sunshine. You look wonderful." He beamed right back at her.

Jackie's entire body was on fire with desire.

Taking her hand, he led her to the car. "Come on, Mom was so excited about you coming, she was up extra early making home made biscuits."

Chad's mother *was* happy at the prospect of seeing Jackie once again. Chad recalled telling her the news.

"Oh, Chad, I'm so happy she came back," his mother had said as she mixed the ingredients for her mouth-watering biscuits.

He decided to speak to his mother about his feelings. "Mom, uhmm, about Jackie, I've been in love with her for a long time, since we were in school together. My feelings never changed over the years. Should I tell her how I feel and hope she'll give me a chance?"

"Chad, you should have told her how you felt ten years ago."

His eyebrows raised in astonishment, he wasn't quite sure what to say.

"Chad, listen. Love is not about color. Your father and I knew what was going on, we knew how you felt about her. She

25

was such a positive influence on you, and we quickly grew to love her. She was a good, decent girl, and I'm certain she grew up to be a fine, decent woman. Her father would have had it no other way. I had always hoped to see you two get married before your father passed away, so he could have seen you as happy as he always believed you would be."

Chad embraced his mother.

"Thanks mom, your feelings mean a lot to me. I'm gone. Be back with her in a jiffy."

***

Victoria Simmons was positively beaming.

"Jackie, look at you! Come here and give me a hug."

"Thank you, Ms. Simmons, you look great, too."

Jackie could see the years had been kind to Victoria. She was still as beautiful as Jackie remembered.

Victoria led her to the table, a table that was filled with just about every breakfast food a person could think of.

"I hope you're hungry. I made it just for you and Chad, and I don't want to hear anything about watching your figure. A man likes a woman with curves, not skin and bones like you see on television."

Jackie looked at all the food. She never was one for eating in the morning, and especially not fried food.

Chad wrapped his arms around her and chuckled, as if reading her thoughts. "Come on, no use fussing," he whispered.

Jackie really enjoyed the breakfast and conversation. She was proud to learn that Chad had built the family business up into a chain of nineteen stores. He had also built a home for himself.

"I wanted to stay near Mom, but I was getting a little to old to still be living with her. So a had a place of my own built on the other side of the pond. I want you to see it."

Chad excused himself to go call his office, and Jackie offered to help clear the table and do the dishes.

"I'm glad you came back, Jackie. You know, Chad's father and myself had hoped you two would get together someday. You two always were good for one another."

Jackie was a bit surprised at Victoria's words. "I always thought you would want someone like Misty for Chad."

Victoria rolled her eyes and patted Jackie's hand. "If you mean because she's white, well, at first we worried that it might be a problem for you two. You know how some people are about mixed couples. But, as time passed, we fell in love with you, too, and didn't care what other people might say. Besides, that Misty isn't the kind of *lady* I want for my son or to be the mother of my grandchildren. When she looks at Chad all she sees are dollar signs and a great piece of ass."

Jackie burst out laughing despite herself.

"Hey, what's so funny?" Chad asked as he came back into the room.

"Girl talk, son," his mother replied.

Jackie gave Victoria a hug, thanked her for the wonderful meal, and promised to visit again soon.

Chad grabbed her towel from the kitchen counter, and said to Jackie, "You can put your swimsuit on at my house."

"See you later, Mom, we love you," Chad said, and gave her a peck on the cheek.

***

Looking around the house, Jackie was amazed. It was a beautiful four bedroom, four-and-a-half bath Colonial style home.

"This isn't your usual bachelor pad," she said, still admiring the tastefully decorated home.

Smiling, Chad walked up behind her and wrapped his arms around her small waist, resting his chin on her shoulder. "Actually, I built this house with the hope of having a family some day."

Having him share his dreams with her reminded Jackie of old times again.

Turning her around to face him, he tilted her chin upwards, letting his fingers rest lightly on her face. His blue eyes burned with such intensity that she found it hard to think.

"Jackie, I want to tell you something, and I don't expect you to answer me now. But please, think about what I do say, alright?"

He ran his hands over his face and sighed. "Damn, I want to say this just right."

Jackie stood wondering what it could possibly be, to have him at such a loss. She took his hand, and gave it a reassuring squeeze. "Just say what you want to say, Chad."

His hands slipped up her arms to rest on her shoulders, he then pulled her closer. "Jackie, I've been in love with you since the seventh grade, and I want you to think about us building a life together."

She started to speak, but he touched her lips with his fingers to silence her. "Don't say anything now, just think about it."

Chad then kissed her, and she was happy to return the kiss with hunger and passion. Their tongues explored one another's, teasing and testing. Her nipple ached for his touch, and it didn't take long for his hands to make their way to her breasts, his long fingers squeezing and gently tugging at her nipples. She wanted and needed more. She pressed her body closer, wanting desperately for him to make love to her right there in the hallway. She was very much aware of his hardness pressed up against her. When Chad finally pulled back she heard herself let out an almost wounded whimper. He rubbed his thumb over her swollen lips and panted, trying to get himself under control, as well.

"Sweetheart, I've dreamed of this for a very long time, and I'll not rush things. If you allow me to have you right now, there's no way in the world that I'm ever going to be able to let you go. So think about it long and hard. I want you for more than just your body and a few hours of pleasure. I want you for good, or never."

He stepped back. "You can change in the bathroom down the hall. I'm going to get in my swimming trunks."

He left her standing in the hallway. She smiled and touched her lips, then started towards the bathroom when something caught her eye. She was surprised and pleased to see that there were several old pictures of Chad's family hanging on the walls, but that wasn't what pleased her. What pleased her was that *she* was in all of them.

Just then the doorbell rang. She went to answer the door, expecting to see Robert and his goofy, devil-may-care grin standing there. It was Misty instead. She was busy digging around in a large beach bag, never noticing who it was that answered the door. When she finally did look up, Jackie had to bite her tongue to keep from laughing out loud. Misty's blue eyes were so wide that Jackie was convinced they would pop right out of her pretty face.

"What are you doing here!" she shrieked so loudly that Jackie thought her eardrums would burst.

Her lips were pinched together so tightly it looked as if she'd just sucked on a lemon—an unripe lemon at that. Jackie glared right back.

"I didn't know I needed your *permission* to be here."

Jackie counted to ten silently, proud of the fact that she hadn't slammed the door shut right in the heifer's face. But she couldn't relish the moment, too. She knew she was really getting to Misty.

She couldn't resist the next words she knew were coming out of her mouth.

"If you want to come in, please do. Chad's getting dressed." Jackie flashed her what she hoped was a mischievous smile. *Let her chew on that*, Jackie thought.

Jackie stepped aside to allow Misty in.

"Sunshine, who's at the door?" Chad called from the bedroom.

Again, she couldn't resist. "It's Misty, and she wants t know what I'm doing in your house!" Jackie called back, extra loud.

Misty was turning a lovely shade of red and Jackie believed the woman was on the verge of exploding.

"Misty, what are you doing here?" Chad asked as he came down the stairs, clad only in his red swimming trunks.

Jackie drank in the sight of him, thinking to herself that she could never get tired of admiring his physique.

"What am I doing here? What is *she* doing here?" Misty shrieked, pointing an accusing finger at Jackie. "I would have thought you'd gotten over your jungle fever by now!"

Hearing that, rage spread it's red mantle across Chad's face. He growled, and both woman recoiled in fear. He stalked up to Misty and grabbed her roughly by the arm.

"Ouch, you're hurting me!" she cried, trying to loose herself from his iron grip. She started crying. "How dare you make a laughing stock out of me, with *her*! I' think I've been more than understanding with you. You're sniffing around her like a dog in heat, just like the way you did in school! Your business will be ruined if you keep this up! Just think what people will say when they find out you're messing around with a....a...*black* woman!"

Misty finally shook herself free and stood back, looking very proud of herself. In her mind, she was getting *through* to him with her reasoning.

Jackie stood in stunned silence. She knew that Misty had wanted to call her more than just a black woman, and nearly had.

Chad had heard more than enough. Grabbing her roughly by the arm once again, he snatched the door open and pushed her out.

Standing looking at the door, Jackie wrapped her arms around herself. She knew that some of the things Misty said were true. Times had changed a little, but not much in small towns such as this. People may accept their friendship a little more openly, but could they ever accept the fact that they were lovers? Could they ever accept any children they may have?

"Jackie, look, I'm sorry you had to hear all that shit," Chad said. He looked as if he was on the verge of crying. He took a step towards her, wanting to give her comfort, but she stepped away.

"Chad, you told me I should think about what I want. Misty *could* be right. You may, and probably will, lose everything you've worked so hard to build. You father's company, Chad. We both have a lot to think about. I better change. Give me a few minutes.

Chapter 3

The ride to Potter swimming hole was quiet. Neither of them really felt like talking. Pulling up to the wooded area near where a group of people had gathered, they spied Robert and Kathy sitting on a blanket near the water. Robert was pouring on the charm and, from the looks of it, Kathy was loving every minute of it.

Jackie got out of the car, stood to the side and took off her jeans and blouse, tossing them into the back seat. Her brown swimming suit enhanced her curves.

When Chad came around the car he stopped dead in his tracks. His eyes traveled up and down her body. The brown suit was skimpy and was only a shade darker than her skin tone. He could feel himself getting aroused, she had that effect on him, and looking at her in that getup would keep him in that state. He had to fight the urge to keep from dragging her off in the woods and making love to her. He watched as she undid the braid, allowing her hair to fall down around her shoulders. She was sexy as hell standing there before him. Chad's heart warmed. She had kept her promise about not getting her hair cut, and now it was down past her shoulder blades. When she turned and leaned into the car to get her towel, Chad saw several of the men stop talking, enjoying the view of her round bottom up in the air. As she turned, tossing the towel over her arm, he could feel his possessiveness take over.

"Maybe you should put your jeans back on."

She smiled, batting his hand away from the towel he was trying to wrap around her.

"Why would I do that? We're here to swim and I'm not going swimming with my jeans on. Come on, let's go say hi to Kathy and Robert."

Chad took her hand, sending a clear message to the men still gawking at her that she was off limits.

Robert and Kathy were so busy talking and laughing they didn't notice their friends were standing in front of them. Robert looked up at Jackie and let out a loud whistle.

"Look at you, lady, I have to say you wear that suit well. Or what there is of it."

Kathy stared at him, then reached out, pinching his arm as hard as she could.

"Ouch Kat, what was that for?" he whined as he rubbed his arm.

Shrugging, she crossed her arms under her full breasts.

"You're a pig! Come on, Jackie, let's go talk. You got up so early I missed you this morning."

Kathy jumped up, grabbed her blanket and Jackie's hand and walked off, but not before turning to give Robert a nasty look.

Chad gave Robert a hard look. "What was that all about?

And when did you start calling her Kat? A few days ago you didn't even remember her last name."

Robert got up to open one of the red coolers sitting on the picnic table and take a beer out.

"You want one?" he asked, holding the bottle out for Chad.

Chad shook his head and waited for his friend to answer his question.

"I've been getting to know Kathy. She's fun to be around. So how are things going with Jackie?"

Both men looked over at the women who were sitting back on the blanket, talking. Sighing, Chad leaned against the table.

"Fine, until Misty came over."

Robert smacked a bug off his arm. "That woman is a pain in the ass, and she'll never give up trying to get her meat hooks into you."

Both men laughed, knowing just how determine Misty could be when it came to Chad.

***

"How did it go, Jackie? What are you going to do? Anyone can see that the man still loves you."

Jackie didn't know what she was going to do or even how to answer Kathy's question.

"Misty showed up this morning while I was at Chad's house, and she said some things that I didn't want to think about, or even admit was possible, but some of what she said is right."

Jackie wanted to change the subject, she really didn't want to think about all the bad possibilities if she decided to be with Chad.

"So, what's the deal with you and Robert? I thought you weren't into white men?"

Jackie then reminded Kathy of a disapproving comment about a co-worker dating a white man. This had happened years earlier.

Remembering her statement years ago, she gave Jackie a sly look, and simply giggled.

"First off, I never said I wasn't into white men, I just said that it was crazy to get into a serious relationship because of the battle the couple has to face. And you know with age comes wisdom. I now think that if you love someone, why not be with them? Also, I've never came across a white man that did much for me. Besides, we're just getting to know one other as friends, that's it."

Jackie chuckled. Surely Kathy didn't think she was fooling her!

She hugged her dearest friend and decided to have some fun with her.

"Really? Well,watching you with him and you eating up all that famous Robert Buckland charm that he's laying on you, I thought I saw some interest between you two."

Kathy didn't say anything, but her silence spoke volumes. Jackie knew she had hit the nail on the head, her friend *was* interested in Robert.

"Okay, Kat, but you have to admit, Robert is not bad looking...for a white boy."

Kathy threw her head back and laughed, then shoved her friend playfully. "I'm going to miss you."

Just then Kathy spotted two men headed their way. She leaned over, to whispering to Jackie.

"Oh, no! Don't look now, but do you remember the yuck twins, Jerry and Joe? Well, they're heading this way."

Jackie remembered them well. They reminded her of the characters Gilbert and Lewis in that old eighties movie,

"Revenge of the Nerds." And they were indeed making a bee-line straight towards them. Both of the men wore their long black hair slicked back. The slick look may have worked for Pat Reilly, but it did nothing for them. Jackie wrinkled her pert nose.

"Be nice, Kat."

Both women put on their best fake smiles, and greeted the twins.

***

Chad and Robert sat watching the women talking and hugging.

"What's your plan? Kat told me Jackie's leaving Monday morning."

Chad had known she only came for the reunion, but he had pushed it from his mind, worrying only about telling her he loved her. Something clicked in Chad's mind, then he turned to look at Robert.

"You came over here with Kathy? Oh man, please don't do her like you do women you deal with. She's not that kind of woman. And if you use her, Jackie might hold it against me."

Robert gave him a look he did not understand, then sighed. "No big deal, just keep calm. But yes, I did come here with her. I would never hurt her. She's great. Stop worrying. Now, what about Jackie?"

Chad tossed a few pebbles onto the ground. "I don't know…I just know I can't let her walk out of my life again. Rob, I know she loves me, she always has, just like I have always loved her. I don't know why she's holding back and fighting so hard to deny what she feels. It's almost like she's afraid to love me."

Robert nodded towards the direction of Kat and Jackie, seeing them talking with two men.

Getting up from the bench, Robert said, "Come on. Can you believe Jerry and Joe are trying to pick up our women?"

"Our women?" Chad questioned with his brow raised. He then burst out laughing at Robert's reaction.

Robert gave Chad a cat that got caught with the canary in his mouth look. "Yeah well, you know what I mean. She came here with me, so I have the right to not want another man all up in her face."

Jackie and Kathy were doing their best to be nice to Jerry and Joe. "No we can't go to dinner with you, but thanks Joe."

Kathy was trying her best to look serious, all the while having to bite her lip in order to pull it off.

"You sure, Jackie? We could play chess and have some wine," Jerry said, trying his best to be suave.

Jackie and Kathy gave each other an amused look, and keep their fake smiles plastered on their faces.

"Sorry guys, their dance card is full for today—and tonight. They'll have to pass on your invitation," Robert growled.

The four people sitting on the ground looked up to see two very intimidating males who didn't look happy.

Smiling back at the twins, Kathy touched Jerry's arm. "We're sorry, guys, but we did make plans with Chad and Robert."

Jackie nodded and smiled at Joe. She felt bad for them, but she could tell that Robert and Chad were making them uncomfortable.

Robert sat next to Kathy, making it clear to the men that they should back off. Kathy glanced at him, then looked at Joe,

Smiling sweetly, she said, "I really wish I would have known you wanted to go out. I wouldn't have made plans. Well, maybe we *could* do something another time. But, at least for today, we're stuck with *them*."

After Jerry and Joe left, Robert turned to Kathy, frowning in disbelief.

"You would rather spend time with Joe than me?"

Kathy smiled, enjoying his reaction. She leaned back and rested her weight on her forearms.

"What can I say? They were going to offer us a fun-filled night of chess and wine."

Robert gave her a wicked smile and pulled her to him, wrapping his strong arm around her waist. "Darling, I can give you a full night."

Slowly and seductively, his gaze slid down her body, then back into her soulful brown eyes. "I'll play with your chest and make you whine…for more."

Moving closer to him, enjoying his flirting, she wiggled her shoulders as if her body was trembling at his words. "Promises…promises. Of course, I could make you do more than whine, baby," she said. She was feeling bold, and part of her hoped he would give her a chance to show that she meant what she said.

When she looked away from a stunned Robert, she noticed Chad and Jackie were smirking and watching them closely. She pushed Robert away, trying to appear unaffected by Robert's open flirting.

"Let me go. I'll get some sandwiches and drinks from the cooler."

Chad held up his hand to stop Kathy from getting up.

"Oh no, you stay put and do that cute couple thing you're doing."

Chad bent down, offering Jackie his hand. "Come on, sunshine, let's leave these two alone."

The day was perfect. The four of them played around in the water, posed for pictures and enjoyed the food that Kathy had prepared for them. As nightfall came they huddled together at a large bonfire that some of the men had built in the clearing. They huddled together laughing and talking with classmates they hadn't seen since leaving school.

Misty spotted the couples, her bitterness and hatred boiling over as she watched Jackie lean against Chad. They looked like they were meant to fit together, almost like together they made a whole. Bile rose in her mouth as Chad caressed Jackie's arm as if he was touching a priceless object. Misty's heart dropped when he kissed her neck. How could he do that? Kiss her in front of everyone? She knew all her years of waiting and dreaming of a wonderful life was wasted, and for that she wanted someone to pay and hurt like she was hurting.

She wanted Jackie to leave town and go back to wherever in the hell she had been all these years, and leave Chad alone. Misty felt that if she had a bit more time, she could make Chad see that she was the woman he needed to make him happy, not Jackie. She was to the point of snapping when she saw Robert whisper something in Kathy's ear and then laugh when Kathy seemed to be embarrassed by what he had told her.

What did the men see in these women? Both Chad and Robert were good looking and successful and they could have just about any woman they wanted, so why did they want Jackie and Kathy?

With false courage fueled by too much alcohol, she charged toward the couples with her three friends following closely behind her.

"Robert! Not you, too! I mean *really*, what's wrong with you and Chad?"

Misty looked around to make sure that everyone heard what she had to say. She hoped to embarrass Jackie so badly that she would leave. Her friends smirking was all she needed to encourage her to keep up the verbal attack.

Jackie and Chad could tell this meeting was going to get out of hand if they didn't put a stop to it. They both stood, hoping that they could defuse the ugly situation. Kathy got up and stood in front of Misty, ready to defend her friend. Shaking his head and standing, Robert stood behind Kathy, thinking of how a perfectly fun time was going down the toilet.

Kathy growled at Misty. "Misty, give it a rest! Why don't you slink off with those buddies of yours and let us get back to our fun?"

Kathy's fists were balled, and she was trying her best not to knock the snotty blond upside the head. She believed in talking out her differences, but some people only understood a hard kick in the ass.

Robert put his hand on Kathy's tense shoulder, giving her a gentle squeeze. She looked up at him, her beautiful brown eyes glowing with anger. *God, there is nothing sexier than a woman with passion*, he thought.

"Baby, ignore her nasty mouth," Robert said calmly.

He smiled down at her as if Misty's nasty comments didn't bother him. But in truth, he was doing his best to hide his anger. He found himself wishing Misty, was a man because he would have loved to knock the hell out of her. But he had never hit a woman, and wasn't going to start now.

Chad looked at Misty, then to her friends, who were eagerly waiting for a bloodletting. He spoke to her in a voice that could chill anyone to the bone.

"Misty, get lost. Who I choose to be with is my own damn business. You're not going to mess up my time with Jackie."

Chad wrapped his arm around Jackie's waist, pulling her close to him, making it clear who he wanted to be with.

Misty knew from the hardness in Chad's voice that she shouldn't push it any further, but, knowing that everyone was witnessing her shame, Misty refused to leave until she thought she had pushed the issue and saved face.

Turning to her friends she said with a nasty sneer, "I want to know why they can't stick with their own. Isn't it bad enough they're moving into our neighborhood?" She eyed the couples with cold triumph.

Kathy had heard enough, it was ass kicking time! Lunging at Misty, she went into attack mode, grabbing handfuls of Misty's blond mane. She moved so fast that she shocked everyone. She snatched the woman's hair back in forth as if she were wringing a chicken's neck Misty shrieked, and most of the men started cheering on the cat fight. The ear shattering scream shook Robert out of his stunned trance, he grabbed Kathy around the waist lifting her off the ground, trying to dislodge Misty's hair from the death grip Kathy had on her. Kathy refused to be stopped, she wanted to yank the bitch bald.

"You redneck bitch, I'm gonna snap your neck!" she screeched, then tightened her hold on the woman's blond locks.

Robert had to bite his lips to keep from laughing, after all, Misty deserved every bit of it. He couldn't believe the trash that has came out of the woman's mouth. Looking at Chad he said, "Uh, little help here?"

He was pulling trying to pull Kathy away, but she was kicking and cursing like a sailor. Chad grabbed Kathy's hands and managed to wrench them loose from Misty's hair, then he pushed the whimpering Misty a safe distance away.

Robert had to strain keep a hold on Kathy, she was fighting like a wild cat to get at the target of her anger. Hefting Kathy higher in his arms, he growled at Misty. "Unless you want that bad bottle-blond dye-job ripped out of your damned head, you better leave while your ass is still in one piece."

41

Still whimpering, Misty looked around and realized that a large group had gathered around her, and most of them were laughing outright at her, while others were trying to hide their looks of amusement.

Gathering what was left of her pride, she smoothed her wild hair on her tender head. She held her red face high, doing her best not to show her shame, and walked away. Her friends followed close behind her, trying to be supportive, but mostly thankful that it was Misty who had to endure the attack and not them.

Robert waited until Misty was safely out of Kathy's grasp before he released his hold. Smiling, he shook has head. He admired her spunk, she was the kind of woman he liked. She was intelligent, funny, she didn't mind kicking a little ass if she needed to, not to mention the fact that the little spit-fire was cute as hell.

He threw his arm around her shoulder. "Woman, you're a firecracker, and I love it!"

Kathy shook a fistful of long blond hair from her hands and wrinkled her nose. She looked up Robert and gave him a sexy smile that made his body tingle.

"You better believe it, baby. That cow better watch that mouth…next time I'll open up a serious can of whoop ass on her. She can think what she wants, but she's not going to stand up and say that stuff to my friend and think she can get away with it. Damn, I should have punched her in the mouth."

Robert chuckled. He had a feeling that getting to know Kathy would be fun, and he did plan on getting to know her better.

Embarrassed, Jackie had had enough fighting for one night. She had always done her best to walk away from confrontations, and she refused to let Misty know that she had hurt her feelings by her racist remarks. But deep down the words really did sting, and it made her realize that she and Chad would have to face people like Misty. She didn't think she could deal with that for the rest of their lives.

"Let's just go, Kat. I don't want to deal with any more crap tonight," she said, looking in the direction that Misty had stumbled off to. Bending, she started gathering her things. She feared if she stayed to long she would burst out in tears in front of everyone.

Chad reached down and gently grabbed her arm to stop her. He knew that if he left her go now she would shut him out again and there would be no getting her back.

"We shouldn't have to leave, we did nothing wrong. But if you want to leave I'll take you back to Kathy's."

Yanking her arm from his grip, she continued to pick up her things. "No! I've had enough for one night. You stay here and enjoy yourself."

Kathy threw her hands up in the air in frustration. She couldn't understand why Jackie felt she had to leave. She, herself, wasn't the type to back down, and she wished Jackie could be the same. Why should they let Misty put a damper on their fun?

"Oh, come on, Jackie, why do you let her get to you?"

Jackie knew by the look on Kathy's face that she wasn't ready to leave.

Chad took her towel and spoke to her softly. "Come on, I'll take you back to Kathy's house, let her and Robert enjoy the rest of the night."

He was determined not to allow her to put distance between them. Not again.

Throwing up her hands, she gave in. She *did* feel bad about asking Kathy to leave.

"Fine, let's go, I just want to leave," she said, snatching up her things. Her frustration was obvious.

Robert gave Chad the thumbs up sign, while Kathy smiled and winked at Chad. She looked like an excited child at Christmas, and she hoped that Jackie and Chad would finally moved forward with their feelings. She felt encouraged when Jackie allowed Chad to take her hand and lead her to his car.

On the drive Chad could feel the tension settle around him like a heavy blanket. He tried to talk to her, but all he got was one-word answers or stiff nods. When he pulled up to Kathy's little house he knew he had to make her open up to him.

"Sunshine, we need to talk about this. Please don't let some small minded bitch mess up what we could have."

Jackie looked at him with tears filling her eyes and shook her head. She then blurted out words that cut her heart, but she knew she had to say them. "We don't have anything, Chad, we never did. It's just not meant to be, please let it go."

She got out of the car hoping that he would accept her weak denial, because she was fighting to keep from giving in and telling him just how much she loved him.

He got out of the car and around to where she stood in a flash, and stepped in front of her.

"I meant what I said Jackie! I don't give a damn about what people will say, and I can't let you just leave me...not again. What do I have to do to make you understand that I love you? How many times do I have to say that I've loved you since we were kids?"

Jackie stomach churned, and she feared she would get physically ill from the anxiety and frustration. She knew she cared so much for him that she would always feel like a part of her was missing if she left him for a second time. But she couldn't be the one to make him lose everything he worked for, because of his love for her.

"I'm leaving Chad, and that's for the best." Her voice broke slightly as she rushed to get the words out, hoping that what she said convenience him and herself that what she said was really what she wanted.

He felt that heartbreaking pain that he had suffered years before. "So, I guess I'm the only one who's in love." His voice was a whisper, yet held a cold edge to it. Chad's words stung like a hard slap. How could he not see how her decision was hurting her, too?

Looking up at him she wanted to tell him the truth but couldn't. She blinked back the tears she feared would fall. His large hand reached out, pushing a stray lock off her face. He needed to feel her soft lips against his. Leaning down he brushed his lips against hers, and felt some hope when she parted her lips and returned his gentle kiss. Putting one hand to her waist, he drew her body to him, the other hand winding around her long neck. When she moaned he deepened the kiss, he wanted to swallow her whole.

She locked herself into his embrace, wanting to feel more of him. She rubbed her body against him, almost instantly arousing him. She could feel him grow hard against her. Chad knew if they kept the passionate kiss up he wouldn't be able to stop, and he wanted to her to understand that he wanted her completely, and not just for sex. Reluctantly, he ended the kiss. Burying his face in her hair he inhaled, taking in her fresh clean scent.

He whispered to her, "I have to go into the office tomorrow, but only for a few hours. I'll come and see you after I'm done and we'll make some plans."

Jackie looked at him, she knew that look, the stubborn set of his jaw and the look in his blue eyes said that he was not giving up. She knew there was no use arguing.

Jackie muttered uneasily, "You're not giving me much choice, are you?"

Running his hand through her hair, he replied, "No, I'm not. I can't let you go. I *won't* let you go, sunshine."

Turning, she started up the wooden porch stairs, but stopped when she heard him call to her. She turned back around.

"Do you love me?"

She gave him a slight smile and she nodded her head. "Yes, I do. Now go home."

She had to laugh when he did a little victory dance and then trotted to his car. Waving to her, he got in and drove off.

She took a long, loving look at him, then turned and went inside, where depression soon overtook her.

Chapter 4

Jackie finished packing her clothes.

Checking her watch, she took her bags out to the rental car that had been delivered an hour before. She wasn't looking forward to the hour long drive to the airport, she knew it would be a long, painful, and lonely drive. She was sure she would spend the whole drive questioning her own decision.

When she finished securing her bags, she went back into the house to say goodbye to Kathy. Knocking on her friend's bedroom door, she called to her. Hearing soft mumbling, she chocked back a laugh as she heard more fumbling behind the door. Kathy cracked the door, doing her best to try and hide her bed mate.

Her short hair was in disarray, she was wrapped only in her white bed sheet.

"You…ummmm, look rested, Kat." Jackie bit her lower lip to try and keep from smiling.

Kathy fumbled with the sheet, unable to hide her pleasure. "Guess I'm busted. Where are you going this early...Is Chad here?"

Jackie looked down at her feet. When she lifted her eyes, the pain was obvious. "I'm catching a flight home. I think it's for the best, Kat. I have a rental car outside."

Jackie heard more movement coming from the bedroom.

Kathy gave her a sheepish look as Robert pulled the door open. He was dressed only in a pair of blue jeans shorts, his chiseled chest was bare.

"You're not leaving again without talking to Chad are you? It'll kill him." Robert ran his hand through his rumpled brown hair, his sleepy green eyes held concern for his friend.

Jackie stood staring blankly at him and then spoke. "I tried to tell him last night that I think it really it's for the best that I just leave. Robert, I have a job and a home to get back to. It was nice to hope for a little while that we could have something special, but it's time to get back to the real world."

Robert rested his chin on Kathy's head, feeling he had to plea on his friend's behalf. "He's been in love with you for so long. He waited for you to come back. Please, *please* give him a chance to talk to you before you leave."

Jackie's heart was breaking, and seeing Robert's sad green eyes pleading for his friend didn't help matters. But she stood firm, shaking her head. "I have to go. Kat, I'll call you when I get home."

Taking Kathy's hand in hers and fighting tears, she kissed her on the cheek. She smiled sadly at Robert, looking in his eyes. "I think he's a keeper, Kat."

Kathy looked up at Robert and smiled. No one had to tell *her* that she had finally met a man who really made her feel special. She knew it was to soon to put much into the things she was feeling for Robert, but she was going to explore them. She smiled to him and then to Jackie, showing her agreement to her friend's comment.

Jackie leaned over and gave Robert a kiss on his cheek. "Be good to her. Take care of Chad for me."

She gave them both a final hug and turned and left the house, not looking back. She was certain that if she *did* look back, she would never leave.

***

As Robert sat on Kathy's couch waiting for Chad, he thought about how Chad would be crushed. *How can she do this to Chad?* he thought to himself. He couldn't help but to be a little angry at her for just leaving and hurting his friend again.

He smiled up at Kathy as she handed him a drink. He took her hand and pulled her down next to him.

"What do you think Chad will do? Will he give up?" Kathy asked. She couldn't hide the worry in her voice. She rested her head on his broad shoulders and placed her hand on his forearm.

He covered her hand with his own, wanting to make her feel better. "Well, the reunion wasn't a total bust. After all, *we* got together." He put his arm around her shoulder and pulled her to him and gave her a soft kiss on her full lips.

Even though he was upset with Jackie, he could understand some of her concerns. Even though he was the one who told Chad he shouldn't worry about the racial concerns that they would face, he knew that he would have to deal with his father, and his possible rejection of Kathy. But he would deal with anything that they would potentially face. His thoughts went back to Chad.

What would Chad do? Could he move on, without the one woman he had loved for so long?

Robert remembered when he and Chad had returned from Europe and Chad found out about her father's death. She had sold her house, and left without saying goodbye to anyone, but Kathy and her family.

Chad had tried many times to contact Jackie only to find out she had changed colleges, going to another across the county. Crushed, Chad had confessed his feelings to Robert, and after a while Chad gave up on trying to contact her. He went community college as he had planned, and took over running the family business. Even though he had had his share of women, none of the relationships lasted for more than a few months.

Robert and Kathy felt sudden dread as they heard a knock on the door, knowing it would be Chad.

Kathy went to the door, opened it, and saw Chad smiling. In his hands was a large bouquet of wild flowers. He knew that they were Jackie's favorite.

Seeing him standing there smiling brightly, Kathy's heart broke for him.

Totally unaware of Jackie's departure, he smiled and hugged Kathy. It was hard for him *not* to show his happiness.

"Ummmm, hi, Chad, come on in." Kathy turned, leading him into her small den. She put her hand on her stomach, hoping to quell the churning. She didn't want to be the one who broke the news to him that Jackie was gone.

Chad had rushed through the work he had at his office, hating every second apart from Jackie. Following Kathy into the room, he was surprise to see Robert lounging on the couch. It was obvious he had spent the night. He was still wearing the same cloths from the day before.

"Well, well, what are you doing here, or do I even have to ask?"

Chad smiled. He should have seen the attraction between them, just from the way they were acting the night before, but he thought they were just being friendly. Looking at them now, well, they *did* make a nice couple.

He gave them an approving smile as Kathy took a sat next to Robert, resting her hand on his leg.

"No, you don't have ask, but I'll tell you. I'm spending time with my lady," Robert said, giving Kathy's hand a squeeze.

"Speaking of ladies, where's Jackie?"

Kathy and Robert both blurted out at the same time, "She's gone."

Chad looked at them as if he couldn't understand what they had said. "What do you mean she's gone? Where did she go?"

Robert got up and walked over to Chad, and put his hands on his shoulders, trying to offer comfort.

"Listen, I know you're upset, but I *know* Jackie loves you, Chad, I can see it in her eyes. Just give her some more time, she'll come around."

Chad tossed the flowers on the coffee table, then began pacing, running his hands through his hair in frustration. "What, wait ten more years?" His vexation was evident. He continued to pace around the room like a wild animal caught in a cage.

"What do you plan on doing?" Kathy asked. She hurt for Chad's loss. She knew just by looking at the man that he truly loved Jackie. She wanted to do something, anything, to make them happy.

Chad shrugged and threw his hands up in the air. "What *can* I do? I think I'll go to work." He left, feeling defeated and lost.

Kathy got up and wrapped her arms around Robert, enjoying

his warmth. Robert kissed her forehead. They both stood there wondering if time would work things out for Chad and Jackie, and they also wondered if their own budding romance would work.

Chapter 5

Jackie returned to work, and just like she had before the reunion, she tried to fill the void in her life by throwing herself completely into it. In the five weeks since the reunion she had taken on three large accounts, with the help of her co-worker Lawrence Webber. The clients were very impressed with her work, and Lawrence had been a big help for her as she tried her best to forget about Chad.

Lawrence had a way of making her laugh even when she felt like crying. His greatest quality was he knew not to be nosy in matters concerning her private life, even though it was evident she was in much anguish. She also admired the was he was focused, and his talent was limitless when it came to their business. He often talked about some day owning his own advertising agency, and she believed that he was well on his way to making his dream come true.

"Jackie, why don't we go and have a drink? Maybe some dinner, then dancing. You need to unwind. It's Friday, and you've been working long hours for well over a month."

Jackie settled back in her leather chair, sipping her coffee and rubbing her neck with her free hand. As she looked at Lawrence, she knew he was right. But she *needed* to work to forget what she had walked away from, for the second time no less. She had walked away from the man that she loved.

"No, I want to wrap up this account by Monday." Stretching, she gave him a lazy smile. "Besides, tagging along would mess up a player like you."

She remembered the last time they went dancing. He had woman throwing themselves at him and giving her nasty looks, thinking she was his latest woman.

Lawrence chuckled and shook his head. "Player? Please woman, *never*! I'm just a man that loves to spending time with beautiful women." He had the nerve to give her an innocent look and batted his long lashes. Knowing there was no use in pushing her, he tossed his hands up as he headed out the door.

Jackie watched him leave. Lawrence was not fooling her, he was a man that loved having many female admirers. Looking at her watch, she picked up the phone and dialed Kathy's number.

She smiled when she heard her friend's bubbly voice.

"Hi, Kat. How are you?"

She heard voices, and what sounded like Robert's full-hearted laughter.

"Jackie, hi! I'm good, we're having a cook out and a few friends are joining us."

Jackie leaned back, cradling the phone with her shoulder as she checked some of her paperwork.

"Oh, sorry for disturbing you, I just thought I'd call while I'm taking a break. Everything going okay with you and Robert?"

Kathy laughed with childlike delight, and Jackie could picture her friend's face beaming with happiness.

"Yes, things are good. No, I take that back, they're great! I'm taking him to meet my family soon."

Jackie was happy things were going well for her friends, but a bit envious that she was too afraid to take a leap of faith and have a life with Chad. She knew Kathy was waiting for her to ask about Chad.

"Is Chad doing okay? Have you seen him?"

Kathy hesitated, then spoke. "Sad, and working his butt off. We tried to get him to come over tonight, but he said he had to work."

Jackie's boss, Maxwell, stood in the door and she waved him in. "I have to go, give everyone my love."

Kathy promised she would call to tell her how the family meeting with Robert went.

Maxell was part owner in the company, he had taken a chance and picked her over other candidates that came from great Ivy League schools. Maxwell had always been her biggest supporter, and he never regretted the decision to hire her.

"Jackie, we may have a new client, and I want you to handle this account, this would be a good boost for us. The company is fast growing and I'd like for us to grow right along with them."

Maxwell glanced at his watch and then looked back at her, his sharp green eyes seemed to be studying. After a moment, he plowed on. "The company owner will be here Monday, and you have been requested by him personally to handle the account."

Jackie tapped her pen on the stack of files she had in front of he, and looked at her cluttered desk. She wondered if she should take on so many clients at one time, but one more client would be one step closer to the top. "Sure I'll be happy to take it. Can I get some background info? Why did he ask for me?"

Maxwell took the seat in front of her, and smoothed back his salt and pepper hair. "Well, as for the background, the owner wanted me to wait until he's here on Monday, so he can personally give you any information you might need. You know how some clients like to get a feel for the people they'll be working with. I do know through another client that the company is very successful, and they're getting ready to open up several more stores. I plan on getting a few more of my best people to work on the account with you, but I want you to heading this project. As for why he wants you, well, you're damn good. You're gaining a reputation for doing top quality work. Enjoy the spotlight, kiddo, you deserve it. Now go home. You're too young and pretty to be working all the time. Go relax, and be here Monday rested and ready to blow this guy away."

He gave her a concerned look. She could tell he wanted to say something but decided against it.

Grunting, he got up and left.

Jackie watched him walk. She was amused by his comment about her working too much. Maxwell would live at the office if his wife would allow it.

A rumbling in her stomach made her give in to his advice to leave. Grabbing her files, she put them in her briefcase and left to find a fast meal before heading home.

***

The following Monday she rushed directly into the conference room, it wouldn't do for her to be late. She had stayed up late the night before to finish the work she had carried home with her over the weekend. She was relieved to see that her new client wasn't there yet.

Lawrence gave her an approving look and handed her a soda. "You look good. Is that for me, or is it to impress our new client?"

Jackie rolled her eyes at him, looking down at her tailored gray pants and white silk shirt. She shook her head, causing her long ponytail to bounce. "I always dress this way, and you know that you silly man. Have you met the new client?"

Lawrence shook his head and smoothed his silk tie as he began to pulling papers out of his briefcase.

Sitting down next to Lawrence she popped open the soda, and was taking a huge gulp just as the conference room door opened. When she saw who came in behind Maxwell, she gasped as the drink was going down, causing her to choke.

Jackie jumped up and bent over trying to catch her breath. Lawrence was at her side in a flash, pounding on her back. Maxwell rushed to the table, wondering what was wrong with her.

"You okay, Jackie? You need some water?" Lawrence asked her.

He was leaning over her, rubbing her back. Anyone could see that he cared about her.

Shaking her head, her cheeks burned in embarrassment, she tried to laugh it off.

"I think I surprised Miss Williams. We were friends years ago. I'm sure she didn't expect to see me."

His words were cool and clear as ice water, and the look on his face made everyone look from Chad to Jackie in curiosity.

Chad didn't notice, as he was too busy watching Jackie and the handsome black man that had his hand on her back.

Maxwell made the introductions to the rest of the staff, then he turned the meeting over Chad, letting him tell the group what he expected of the firm and some of his ideas. He listened to the input that everyone had, and when Lawrence spoke Chad regarded him coolly.

Jackie put all her effort into listening to the ideas being put out, but she was having a hard time keeping her mind on her work.

As the long and uncomfortable meeting came to an end, Jackie assured Maxwell and Chad that she would have the preliminary ads ready by the end of the week.

Maxwell stood up, signaling the meeting was over. He told everyone to let the two old friends catch up.

Lawrence was the last to leave, turning to Jackie and touching her shoulder in a protective manner. "I'll be in my office if you need me."

He nodded to Chad as he left the room, turning again to look at Jackie just before shutting the door.

Jackie had to fight the urge to run out of the room right behind him. Instead, she started gathering her papers, putting them in her briefcase. As the seconds passed in dead silence she became uncomfortable, wishing he would say what he had to say and leave. She looked up and faced Chad's cold stare.

"Is he the reason you left me? Is he the reason you wouldn't consider me for the man in your life?"

His expression was one that she had never seen directed at her, anger and disappointment. Jackie looked away from him for a moment and then back to him and sighed. "No, he's not why I left. I had to get back to my job. I had a life that I wasn't willing to give up."

She hoped that he would believe what she was saying.

His gaze was hard, it made her want to look away. But she knew if she backed down he would see that as giving in to what he wanted, and she was resolved that he wouldn't change her mind.

Even with anger scrawled on his face, Chad looked wonderful in his black business suit with a burgundy tie. He looked sexy, and had a sexual magnetism that made him look so self-confident. She felt a moment of panic run through her. Having him so close was overwhelming, she needed her distance.

"Why are you here, Chad? There are firms closer to your home."

Walking towards her, Chad moved with the grace of a big cat stalking his prey.

He's moving in for the kill her mind screamed.

"I think you know why I'm here, sunshine, don't you?"Reaching out, he began caressing her face.

Her senses reeled as if her body was short circuited. She had to force herself to regain control. "Chad, I have to get back to work...and..."

His mouth descended and covered hers, putting an end to her weak refusal. The kiss devoured her like a man feasting on his last meal.

She couldn't put up a fight, and suddenly she didn't *want* to stop him. Wrapping her arms around his neck, she pulled him closer, feeling her body into his.

That was all he needed. Chad pulled her closer and put all his passion into the kiss. His hand roamed down her back and then came to rest on her hips. He felt her body shudder.

Fighting the urge to push her on the table, make love to her and claim her as his own, he slowly, and forcibly, calmed himself.

Jackie finally gained control of her raging urges and pulled back, although both of them were panting and unable to hide the desire in their eyes.

He liked the way her lips were swollen from his rough kiss, her hair wildly arranged around her shoulders from where he had pulled the ponytail holder from her hair.

"I came to get you, and I'm not leaving unless you're with me." His words were so final that it almost sounded as if he would take her no matter what. Willing or unwilling.

Huffing, she looked around for her ponytail holder. She spotted it on the floor and picked it up, and hurried to put her hair back into a not-so-neat ponytail. She grabbed her briefcase from the table and turned to leave, but he stepped around her and stood in front of her, blocking her from the door.

His blue eyes darkening, he said, "I'm tired of you running. You did it ten years ago and you're doing it now. I'll come back for you tonight. We can go to dinner and we're going to start making plans like we should have made a long time ago."

He turned and left, leaving Jackie standing in the conference room, dumbfounded.

***

Jackie spent the day not only dodging questions from fellow co-workers, but questioning looks as well. At the end of the day she took refuge in her office, sank into her large leather chair, leaned back and propped her feet up on the desk.

Lawrence knocked lightly on her door, and she looked up to see him wearing a smug smile. Coming into the office, he sat on her couch and crossed his arms, but said nothing. It was evident that he was waiting for her to speak. It didn't help her mood at all.

"Something you need?" she snapped at him, knowing full well what he wanted to know.

His eyes twinkled with amusement. "I had to go through the office gossip gauntlet, and you should have heard the barrage of questions from all the single women. Hell, even a couple of single *men*. The overwhelming majority simply wanted to know who that "hunk of a man" was."

"And what I want to know is this. Is he the man you've been in love with all this time? For all these years?" His voice was soft, his eyes full of compassion.

Jackie sighed and closed her eyes. "Is it really that obvious?"

"Jackie, a blind man can see the chemistry going on between you two. What I want to know is, why aren't you two married, if you feel that way? It makes no sense."

Slightly surprised, she opened her eyes and looked at him closely. "It doesn't bother you, the fact that he's white? I mean, I just assumed that most black men would resent that. Hell, even a lot of *white* men would."

His face took a serious, stern look. "Of *course* some folks would have a problem with the race thing. But you know what? I say to hell with them. Honey, if you love the man, then just worry about the two of *you*, not everyone else. Just face whatever life may throw at you, just do it *together*."

Getting up, she strolled over to the window and looked out.

"I've told you about my father Lawrence, but what I *didn't* tell you was this. My dad drank himself to death, heartbroken over my mother. She left him when I was only nine years old. He did his best for me and loved me dearly, but I think that sometimes it hurt him just having me around also, because I reminded him of her."

Sucking in her breath she continued, unsuccessfully fighting back her tears. "The day after I buried my dad I was going through some of his things, you know, packing some stuff. I came across an old letter written to him, from my Mother. It was written the same day she left us. All she said was that she wanted more out of life than just being a wife and mother, and that love just wasn't enough. That was it. She simply walked out on us, the two people who loved her more than anyone in the world. She said love wasn't enough."

She looked at Lawrence with such pain in her eyes, it was all he could do to keep from crying himself.

"Lawrence, what more could a person want? Dad was a good man, a hard worker, and would have did anything in the world, *anything,* to make her happy. But I saw first hand what love can do to a person. It can take a person to the heights of heaven, or it can take a person to the depths of hell. How can I, how can *anyone,* take a chance like that? I mean, my mother *did* vow at one time to stick with him through sickness and health, for better or for worse. I made a promise to myself a long time ago to never let a person hurt me the way my father was hurt. So I sold the house, went to college, and worked hard to build a life of my own. And here we are. I just want to have my own safe, comfortable existence back. That's all."

Lawrence had never seen Jackie like this. Ever. She was always guarded and controlled, but now she looked like a lost little girl. He did the only thing he could think of to do for his friend, he went to her and embraced her warmly and protectively. He kissed the top of her head as she let the tears flow freely.

"Sweetie, what she said was a weak ass excuse. Have you ever thought that maybe she just didn't value what she had with you and your father? Or maybe she just wanted out and didn't have the guts to be honest with your father? For some people it's better to blame others than to be truthful to themselves. Don't let what your mother did keep you from being happy."

Jackie buried her face in his chest. Part or her knew what Lawrence said was right, all she had to do is put all her past hurt behind her. But could she do that?

Thankful she had a friend that supported and loved her, she wrapped her arms around him. Lawrence had become like a brother to her.

Chad stood, watching Jackie and Lawrence, feeling somewhat hurt. He wanted to snap the man's arms, but he was already on shaky ground with Jackie, and causing a scene at her office by attacking the man would only make things worst.

"Am I interrupting anything?"

They both turned to look at Chad. Jackie stepped out of her friend's embrace.

"No, you haven't," Lawrence stated matter of factly, then smiled down at Jackie, winked at her, and whispered, "Good luck. I'll call you later, Jackie, to check on you."

He strolled out of the office, hoping Jackie would overcome her fear and give Chad a chance. He had to admit when he first met Jackie he did want to date her, but she made it clear she was not looking for anything but friendship, and for the first time in his life he had a close female friend. He held no grudge, and was thankful Jackie had become someone he could truly rely on.

Lawrence's cool behavior ruffled Chad. It was obvious to him that Jackie had a close relationship with the man, but how close?

"You know, I really hate seeing another man, that man, holding you. Damn, Jackie, I want to know what's going on with the two of you!" Chad growled.

Jackie gave him a chilly look, and her brown eyes narrowed. If looks could kill he would have fell dead on the spot. He had twice accused her of being involved with Lawrence.

"You need to get a grip and drop this Alpha male crap! Do you believe I would let you touch me if I were in a relationship with Lawrence? Better yet, do you think he would leave you alone with me if we did have a relationship?"

He felt like a child being caught doing something bad.

"What am I suppose to think?" he asked, knowing that was a weak response, but that was all he could say that made sense at the time.

Throwing up his hands in frustration, he walked to her and looked down into her lovely brown eyes. Just seeing her eyes twinkle it made his soul soar. He had heard people say many time that they could drown in someone eyes but he had never experienced that until this moment.

"Sunshine, when it comes to you, I don't know a whole lot. However, one thing I *do* know is that I love you, and you love me. Don't deny it. I don't know what's holding you back, I just wish I could get you to open up to me."

He leaned down and kissed her tenderly. When he broke the kiss Jackie looked into his eyes. There was no hiding the lusty look in his eyes, it mirrored her own needs and desires.

"Come on, let's go…I know a great place to have dinner."

She grabbed his hand and snatched her briefcase off her desk, and hurried out of the office.

***

Jackie took Chad to a restaurant that she and Lawrence went to at least three times a week. Val's Vittles was the best soul food and country cooking restaurant in town. The food was great and the atmosphere was always laid back and welcoming.

Chad noticed Jackie had relaxed a bit. She seemed to be a regular by the way the waiter, and even some of the other diners, greeted her.

They enjoyed the dinner, he loved the food, it was the kind of food they both grew up on. He was so happy to just be sitting with her, listening to her tell him about the town and some her favorite place to go when she wasn't working.

She was becoming more like her old self, joking and kidding, even laughing at his silly comments.

He watched as she savored the last bite of her chocolate

cake. He almost groaned aloud as he watched her slowly lick the chocolate frosting from her luscious lips. Chad shifted uncomfortably in his seat. He knew that she was well aware of what she was doing to him, as she put down her fork and scooped up the last of the frosting with her long manicured finger. He felt his body temperature rise as she slowly slid her finger in her mouth and then twirled her finger cleaning the frosting off her finger.

She then had the nerve to bat her eyes, causing her long lashes to fan against her skin, and then she spoke in a fake innocent voice. "Something wrong? You're not eating your dessert." She pointed to his apple pie that he had not touched.

Food was the last thing he wanted at that moment, and she knew that. She was teasing him, knowing full well she was playing with fire. It was taking all his self-control to not drag her out of the restaurant and find a private spot to make love to her.

Chad wished the waiter would hurry and return with his credit card so they could leave. He wasn't in a hurry to end the night, but he wanted to be alone with her so he could express his love to her. He wanted to spend every day of the rest of his life showing her just how much her loved her.

Taking her hand in his, he planted small kisses on her palm that made her shiver. His voice was husky when he spoke.

"Do you know how much I love you? I don't understand this at all. It's been ten years, but I feel as if we never parted ways, that you've been with me the whole time. You do know that I truly love you, don't you?"

Looking into those intense blue eyes was so overwhelming she could only nod, then look away.

Her gaze caught several people staring at them. Most seemed to be merely curious. However, there were three young professional looking black men that clearly wore looks of disapproval. These were the same men she saw when she would come in with Lawrence to have lunch breaks. They had always exchanged polite nods and smiles, but it wasn't like she knew the men. Now all of them were staring at her as if she were a criminal.

Chad turned to see who she was giving such a long hard look at, and spied the young men looking at him with a mixture of mistrust and anger. Just from the looks on their faces he knew what they were thinking. He wasn't foolish, he knew some people would disapprove, and there would people that would be openly hostile towards them. But he also knew that he would be ready to defend and protect Jackie if need be.

Jackie didn't understand their nasty attitudes. On several occasions she had seen all three of them flirting with the young, white waitresses who worked there. Yet they didn't think it was right for a white man to kiss a black woman's hand in public. She didn't understand why they would even care, they didn't even know her. The looks on the men's faces enraged her.

Chad knew what she was thinking, he could feel her anger. The last thing he wanted was her pulling away again, because of a few small-minded people. Gently, he squeezed her hand to get her attention.

When she turned he spoke to her in a low, calm voice. "Sunshine, I'm willing to deal with anyone or any problem, as long as you're with me. So what if people give us looks? What does that matter? This is about you and me, and what I know we can have together, if we just try."

She knew he meant what he said right *now*, but what would he say when things got really hard? What would he do if he started losing business because he was with her? Would he feel like her mother, that she was holding him back from having something better? Would he stand by her side no matter what? Was she willing to risk her heart?

All the questions racing through her mind made her feel sick to her stomach and she feared she would begin to panic. Feeling the need to retreat, she said the first thing that came to her mind. "It's getting late, can you take me home now, Chad? I need to begin working on your ads, anyway."

One of the men, the youngest of the three from the looks of it, decided to approach their table. "Excuse me, sister." He addressed Jackie, not bothering to acknowledge Chad at all.

"I can't understand why you disrespect yourself this way," he said, sweeping his hand out towards Chad.

His voice was full of contempt, and it was quite apparent that he expected an answer from her, and her alone.

Chad stood so quickly that Jackie wasn't able to stop him. Several people had turned around and were staring.

"Disrespecting her? Who in the hell are you to come over here and say that to her? Do you know her, or are you just thinking that a white man will only use her? Well, if you think that, you are sorely mistaken. I've known this woman most of my life, and she has far too much class to be used by *anyone*, white *or* black." Chad spoke softly, but his voice held a rock hard edge that she had never heard before.

She had never seen him so mad. Jackie hoped the scene wouldn't get out of hand. The man wasn't backing down, he just stood glaring at them.

Chad wasn't backing down either, and she knew there was no use in her suggesting they leave quietly. She knew Chad well enough to know he didn't just walk away from confrontations. He would stand his ground and deal with whatever had to be dealt with.

The young man ignored what Chad had said and continued with his rant, pointing at Chad, but still addressing Jackie. "To him you're some curiosity, something he can brag to his friends about. You have to know that no real black man would want you after him."

Now it was Jackie who was jumping up to face the man down, her brown eyes filled with fire. She balled her hands into tight fists to keep from doing violence to the man. "Let me tell you something. You don't know me, so what gives you the right to even suggest I would be with a man, any man, who would not love me and respect me?"

Fighting her anger, she held her head high and met the man's nasty disapproving glare. "This man has loved me since high school. We've been friends for sixteen years, and in all that time he has treated me with nothing but respect. Where do you see disrespect, or me being a curiosity?"

She blew out an angry breath, and was glad to see the waiter come with Chad's credit card.

Chad smiled and took his card from the nervous waiter. He had overheard the conversation, and from the look of Chad, he feared that there would be a fight in the restaurant.

Taking Jackie's hand, Chad smiled down at her. He could not be more proud of her. She had stood and faced the man, and now he hoped that she would have the courage to love him freely and openly.

Giving the man a penetrating look, Chad spoke with pride. "Actually, I've loved her from the first time I saw her in the hallway at school. We were in the seventh grade. That is when she captured my heart."

Jackie smiled up at him, her gaze as soft as a caress. *I love this man.* she thought. Just the thought made her heart race.

Chad didn't give the man another glance as he led Jackie out of the restaurant.

Chapter 6

Robert eased his black Mustang into the driveway of Kathy's mom. Looking at Kathy, he smiled. He knew he was in love with her, because he had never went to meet a girl's parents before, it just wasn't his style.

"You ready for this?" Kathy asked.

She was both excited and nervous, and prayed her mother and brother would like him and accept him.

"Baby, stand back and let me wow the hell out of everyone," he joked as he straightened his silk tie.

Kathy let out a nervous giggle. He had an air of calm and self-confidence that she found irresistible. She watched as he got out of the car and came around to open her door. *My man cleans up nice*, she thought.

Wanting to make a good impression on her family, and much to her pleasure, he showed up at her house looking as if he had stepped out of a magazine. His gray suit fit him perfectly.

Kathy knew that Robert was the kind of man who women drooled over. As a matter of fact she had done her share of drooling the last few weeks. Robert was good looking, but she learned that there was so much more to him than simply good looks. He was passionate, smart, kind, funny, a hopeless romantic, and supportive. Kathy thought he was almost too good to be true, and she was falling deeply in love with him.

Opening the door for her, Robert smiled down at her, his gray eyes twinkling. She overwhelmed him with her spirit and passion, and he couldn't help but wonder if she was the woman that he had been waiting for. No, he *knew* that she was the woman he had been longing for, and now he was ready to tell her and her family just how he felt. Offering her his hand, he helped her out of the car. She smoothed her blue floral dress over her voluptuous body. Hand and hand they walked into her mother's house.

As soon as they stepped into the modest house they knew this was not going to be a happy meeting. Kathy's mother, Valerie, sat in a large Queen Ann chair, Robert thought she looked like a queen holding court. Judging from the hateful and un-welcoming look on her face, his fate had already been sealed.

Kathy's brother, John, was leaning in the doorway, glaring at Robert as if he had committed some indecent act on his sister.

"Momma, John, this is…"

Her mother held up her hand, indicating she wanted silence. "I know who he is, baby."

Nodding her head towards John, Kathy's mother spoke, and her voice had an hard edge to it. "John told me what they call this boy at the mill," she said, all the while shaking her head in disapproval.

Robert's heart sank, he knew his reputation was what Kathy's mother was talking about.

"Ma'am, I'm Robert Buckland. I know your son. He works for my family."

Not wanting to beat around the bush, John stepped forward in front of Robert. Although Robert stood a few inches taller, both men made and intimidating duo, both looking like they were trying to protect what they both thought was theirs to protect, and that was Kathy.

"Kat, they call him...Mr. Hump 'em and Dump 'em Buckland. Did you know that? Did he tell you how he has no shame when it comes to women? Do you know what kind of man you're dealing with, sis?"

Kathy gasped, shocked at her brother's statement. She knew now her mother and brother would never give Robert a chance, and when it come down to it, her family would expect her to make a choice.

Robert glanced over at Kathy, his heart falling somewhere around his feet. He had hoped his past wouldn't be an issue, and even though his past *was*, in fact, of his own doing, he couldn't help but feel angry at John for spilling the beans. Couldn't they tell how much he loved her just by looking at the two of them together? He wanted to beat the living shit out of John, right then and there. *Easy does it now, blowing your cool with them certainly won't help matters*, he thought.

"You know how it is, John. People are always talking, even if they don't know a damn thing about the person they're talking about. There is not one woman I ever dated who ended up saying I used her." Robert knew that was weak, but it was the only defense that he could come up with on short notice. For the first time in his life, Robert *truly was* ashamed of his past actions.

"Tell my baby sister how it is, Mr. Buckland. Tell her about all the notches you have on your desk."

Turning to Kathy, John continued the barrage of mud-slinging.

"That's right, Robert here has had his share of women right in his office, not caring who heard or knew what was going on. Of course, with all the moaning and screaming, you would have to be a fool to *not* know. He has no respect for woman at all, Kat."

Kathy's face burned, and her dark eyes held the tortured dullness of disbelief.

"John, what's wrong, you jealous?" Robert's mouth was pulled into a sour grin.

John didn't see the humor in the comment, and shoved Robert back away from him.

Robert wanted to punch John in the face, even though every word was true. And that made him even madder. Yes, he had been with women at the mill, but he never forced any women to do anything that she didn't want to do. He wished they would give them the chance to prove to them that he would not hurt Kathy, or use her.

Valerie jumped up and grabbed John's arm, trying to keep the situation from spiraling out of control. She feared if the two men went after each other they could do some serious damage to her house, and themselves. Pushing John to the side, she looked at Kathy, her angry look softening as she spoke.

"Kathy, this man is nothing but a dog in heat. You've always been a good, respectable girl, and you've done good for yourself. Are you going to let him drag your reputation through the mud and bring shame on this family? And what happens when he's done with you? No good man will want a woman who has been with him. When he's done he'll go back to his life, and he'll leave your life in a mess. Leave him alone before he hurts you."

Robert pulled Kathy beside him possessively, with very real

affection. "Mrs. Henderson, I'm not looking to hurt your daughter. I care about her."

John let out a snort of disbelief. "Sis, how many women do you think he's said that to, that he cares? He'll say anything to get you into bed, then use you until he finds someone else."

Ignoring the angry look from Robert, John approached his sister and tenderly cupped her face between his hands. "Kat, I'm sorry, but if you let this man use you, then you get what you deserve. You're my sister and I will always love you, but I'm disappointed in you. I can't believe as smart as you are, you fell for his bull. He's a user and that's all he will ever be." John gave her a peck on the forehead, turned, and left the room. He seemed to be pleased with himself.

"I'll call you later, Mama," Kathy whispered, choking back tears.

She blindly stumbled towards the door.

Robert started to speak to her mother, but what could he say? She would only believe he was lying. Following Kathy out of the house, he pulled her into his arms. He felt if he let her go she would run, and never come back to him. He would never let that happen.

"Kathy, baby, I'm so sorry." His heart ached when he looked into her sad brown eyes.

"Just take me home. I don't feel like talking right now, Robert." Kathy's mind was racing. She knew Robert dated a lot of women, but could he be unscrupulous enough to tell her he cared, just to have a fling with her? *He didn't deny any of John's accusations* she thought. *Has he really changed?*

She wanted to reject the thought as being absurd, but she couldn't. What made her more special than any of the other women? There was truth to what her brother said, and she could not be…just another woman.

***

Arriving at Kathy's house, Robert put the car in park, then turned and looked at her. "Kathy, listen to me."

Ignoring him, she keep her gaze out the window, seemingly looking at nothing. After a few moments she turned and asked him a question, point blank, all the while wondering of she really wanted to know the answer. "Is it true Robert, everything John said?"

Leaning his head against the headrest, he rubbed his hand over his mouth and spoke. "Kat, I never said I was an angel, you know that. I never promised any of the women in my past a thing. Hell, they knew it was all about sex. Safe sex, I might add."

Her mouth dropped open, she was stunned by his bluntness. She flung her hands out in a warding-off gesture, not caring to hear about what he did or didn't do—with other women.

"Robert, damn, that is too much information. I just wanted to know if it was true, that you were only after one thing, not if you had safe sex with some woman."

"Kat, that was the past. Hell, I haven't been with anyone since the first time we made love."

Crossing her arms under her full breasts, she looked away from him. "We've only been together for five weeks, Robert. What are you saying, that this is the longest you've been with one woman?"

His heart was slowly breaking. He could hear the subtle mockery in her voice. He decided that total honesty was needed in order to restore her shaken faith in him. If she thought he was sugar coating things, or, God help, caught in even a little white lie, he sensed it would be all over, for good.

"Alright, yes. You've been the only woman I've dated this long, and I'm seeing only *you*. That should say something about how I feel. I'm falling in love with you."

Wanting to reassure her, he leaned over, turned her face to meet his and pressed his lips to hers, caressing her mouth more than kissing.

"Baby, I won't hurt you, you must know that. I promise I'll not to do anything to hurt you in any way." He sealed his vow with another kiss.

Kathy wanted to surrender completely, but her brother's words came rushing back into her mind. Pushing him back, her trembling hands rested on his chest. "Goodbye, Robert. It's been...fun."

She kept her features deceptively composed, but inside her heart was breaking.

Robert sat looking at her, his gray eyes becoming as flat and unreadable as a stone. In a panic, he grabbed her arm, restraining her. "Kat, please don't do this. I can't change my past, but I promise you I'll not repeat the past with you."

She pulled her arm away, knowing that if she stayed any longer she wouldn't be able to walk away.

"Take care of yourself," she said as she got out of the car.

Robert sat stunned, hunched over his steering wheel. He felt he had been punched in the stomach. "Damn! I finally open my heart to a woman and she kicks me in the balls," he mumbled. He wanted to scream at the top of his lungs, but all he could do was shake his head. He would give her time to think, then he would call and beg if he had to. He had to get her back, he just had to.

Chapter 7

Chad had refused to take Jackie back to her car and, after a small argument, she allowed him to drive her home.

Arriving at her house, he smiled at the sight of the neatly manicured lawn. She had several large flowerbeds filled with an assortment of roses and, near a bay window, facing the street, was a huge purple butterfly bush.

Stepping inside of the house, he noticed the décor suited her. It was furnished in mission style furniture, simple and classic.

"Do you like it?" She watched as he took in his surroundings.

Walking over to the stone fireplace, he looked at two pictures in silver frames. One of her standing with her father, taken the day of their graduation. He could see the pride and love in her fathers eyes. The other picture had been taken at Potter's swimming hole. Himself, Robert, Kathy and her.

"I love it, I hope we can make it our home together. This is nice and comfy."

Huffing, she glared at him. "Would you stop that please? I'm not leaving my job and home. Do you realize how hard I had to work to get where I am?"

He stepped up to her and whispered to her, "Baby, I want you so much."

His eyes burning with desire, Jackie felt empowered to see such desire in his eyes, and the need in his voice set her on fire. Walking away from him she began unbuttoning her shirt, giving him a sexy smile. She ran her hands down her full breasts, then slowly down her pants, unzipping and stepping out of them, leaving her in a lacy white bra and panties, her thigh high hose and black high heels.

His eyes devoured her as she slowly turned, making sure he saw every inch of her body. Chad stood trembling with passion as she walked to her bedroom. He loved the way her hips swayed. He had never really worshipped a woman's body before, but at that moment he wanted to fall to his knees and worship her.

Jackie walked into her bedroom, slid down on the bed, and wondered how long it would take for him to follow.

"One…two…"

She giggled when Chad came into the room, watching as he fought to get undressed. He threw his jacket behind him, not caring where it landed. The rest of his cloths came off in a whirl, with the same result, being flung in random directions.

Standing in front of her, he was everything she dreamed he would be. As her eyes drifted down his body, she decided he was more than what she had dreamed of.

His body was hard and lean, and she shook from arousal as she gazed down to his erect and long member. "You are a beautiful man," she said breathlessly.

Smiling, he reached for her high heels, removed them and

began rubbing her feet, slowly making his way up to her thigh-high hose.

Crawling onto the bed he urged her to lie back.

The dim light in the room made her look even more erotic, her hair splayed around the pillow.

So long he had hoped she would be with him, wanting him, he could hardly believe it was happening. He cupped her lovely face.

"I love you so much," he whispered against her lips. His kiss became filled with hunger and need.

Gliding his hand down to her bra, he fumbled with the front clasp and opened it. Having access to her full breasts, he began teasing both of her nipples with his long fingers. Responding to his touch, she moaned and arched her back, offering more of herself to him. He took her dark nipple in his mouth, his tongue flicked and teased it, then nipping it with his teeth, he moved to the other nipple, giving it the same lusty treatment.

Jackie's body felt as if she was electrically charged as his tongue made a slow sensual decent down her body, trailing down to her stomach. Almost giddy with delight, she giggled when he ran his tongue over her bellybutton. Her giggle quickly died when he parted her legs, keeping them apart with his broad shoulders. Chad inhaled her personal scent. It was intoxicating and driving him wild. Planting small kisses all over her wet, throbbing passion, his tongue then danced slowly against her womanhood, sliding deeper into her. Shouting, she begged for him to continued his wonderful assault with his tongue. He knew she was ready to release all her pent up desire. He continued licking, tasting, and teasing her. Her body was trembling. Her release felt like she was free falling. So sensitive to his touch she tried moving away from him, but he held her in place.

"Oh God, Chad, stop," she moaned out loud as her body thrashed.

Thinking she couldn't stand much more of what his tongue was doing to her, she grabbed his hair and pulled him up onto her still-trembling body. His body fitting neatly between her thighs, she squirmed beneath him. He gave her a tender kiss as he slowly slipped into her paradise.

"Oh, God, you feel wonderful!"

Her body gripped him tightly as he moved forward, stopping when he hit a barrier. His eyes grew wide with surprise when he realized what it was.

Cupping her face, he looked into her eyes. "Sunshine...damn, you should have said this was your first time. Baby, stop moving...just give me a minute...ohhhhhhh, please hold still."

Jackie smiled as she watched Chad try his best to keep in control. She squirmed, deliberately trying to drive him over the edge. No longer able to hold back, he thrust deep inside her. Jackie let out a surprised yelp, but quickly her body began to shake with pleasure. She was close to releasing. Wrapping her arms and legs around him and arching her body, she screamed her release. Chad soon followed her, throbbing, his senses reeling. Feeling as if he would pass out, he laid his forehead on hers, both of them breathing heavy.

"Jackie, you make me feel whole. I love you so much."

She snuggled against him, running her hand over his sweaty chest. "I love you. Chad, I do."

Chad wrapped her in his arms, and she fell asleep content.

Chapter 8

Kathy paced her office to work off excess energy, all the while looking at her phone.

For three days she had avoided all of Robert's calls. She refused to open the door when he came to her house. She missed him terribly, and wondered if she had perhaps made a mistake. She wondered if he missed her as badly, if at all.

Seating herself at her desk, she sat thinking. Grabbing the phone she dialed the mill before she lost her nerve.

"Buckland Lumber."

Kathy recognized the gruff voice of Robert's father. Clearing her throat, she rushed to get the words out. "Hi, Mr. Buckland, this is Kathy Henderson, may I speak to Robert?"

She heard the man mumble something and then sigh. "He's not in today. I thought you weren't seeing him anymore?"

Kathy could tell he was hoping his son was done seeing her, a black woman.

"That's between me and Robert. Could you please mind your own business, and please tell me where he is?" Gripping the phone she knew her tone was nasty, but she didn't want to deal with the man's attitude.

"Young lady, listen. You and Robert are better off apart. You both had your fun, now please leave my boy alone. This mixed race stuff is nothing but trouble." His voice was stern, with no vestige of sympathy.

Instead of responding to his insults and unwanted advice, she slammed the phone down. *It's over. Just let it go,* she thought as she blinked back tears she feared would fall. There was no use wishing things were different. With their families against them, it would be hard to have a relationship without the love and support of the ones she loved.

Her phone ringing brought her out of her sad thoughts. She had to work to do and needed to move on.

"Mountain Press, Kathy Henderson speaking, may I help you?"

Grabbing a pad and pen, she was expecting someone calling to order advertising space in the newspaper. She waited for the person to responded.

"Kat...baby, please talk to me."

She could hear Robert's pain, it matched hers. Closing her eyes, she hung up, not saying a word. She then dialed her boss's extension. "Jack...this is Kathy...I need to go home. I'm feeling awful. Must be a virus."

Chapter 9

Jackie woke late for the third day in a row. She rushed to get ready for work, fussing at Chad to leave her alone so she could get dressed.

Each day after work Chad came to pick her up and, like the first night together, their cloths ended up all over the house. She was so into being with Chad she hadn't bothered to even get her car from work in three days.

Forgetting that fact, she rushed outside, only to remember that her car wasn't there. Running back inside she yelled at Chad to get dressed as he laughed.

He stopped at a fast food restaurant, managing to get her to eat breakfast. When she got to work she kissed him goodbye and rushed off.

Jackie smiled as she went to her secretary's desk. She saw she had several messages from a few clients, and three from Kathy. She decided the clients could wait. Going into her office, she tossed her briefcase on the desk, and tried to phone Kathy at work. She was surprised when she was told that Kathy had taken vacation time, and they didn't know how to reach her.

Worried, Jackie called Kathy at home.

When Kathy answered she became even more alarmed at hearing her sniffling.

"Kat, are you okay? Kat, talk to me."

She heard Kathy sniffle again. "Oh, Jackie, I'm alright...just a little upset."

Her voice sounded hoarse from crying.

"Tell me what's wrong, Kat, is your mother okay?" she asked, wishing she could be there to comfort her.

Kathy blew her nose. "Besides hating Robert, yeah, Mom is okay. I took Robert to meet my family and as soon as we got there it was a nightmare. My brother told me everything about Robert's reputation at the mill, and he said that Robert was using me. Oh, Jackie, they almost came to blows. John told me if I kept seeing Robert I would get hurt and I would get what I deserve. That's not all. My mother has tried to set me up with every single black man in town, and the next town. And don't get me going about Robert's father putting his two cent in the mix. He feels that it would be nothing but trouble for his son to be in a mixed race relationship."

Jackie listened and let her friend vent. She was hurting for her, and wanted desperately to give her any help she could.

"Kat, honey, I'm sorry. What can I do to help?"

Kathy spoke in a suffocated whisper. "I told Robert I wasn't going to see him anymore and he's been calling countless times, and keeps coming by." She let out a weak laugh.

"He's just like Chad, he refuses to give up. I was thinking I could come and stay with you. I know Chad is there, but I need to get away."

There was no way she would let Kathy be alone.

"Kathy, don't worry about Chad being here. Tell me when you want to come. I'll be at the airport to get you."

After booking a flight, Kathy called back, saying she would be flying into town the following day at noon.

Gathering all her work, Jackie headed towards Lawrence's office. After tapping on the door she went in, and sat on the edge of his desk.

"Well, you're glowing, Jackie. Or, should I say, you have a lovely afterglow? Nights of loving tend to do that to you."

Shooting him an annoyed look, she handed him her ideas for Chad's store ads. "Can you handle Chad's account? I'm going to take some time off to help out a friend."

Lawrence took the files, then looked back at her, trying to read her. "Something you want to talk about?"

She smiled and shook her head. "No, I just need to help a friend through some things. We'll talk when I get back to work. I have to go talk to Maxwell."

Lawrence wanted to press her for an answer, but knew Jackie well enough to know she would only talk when she was ready. He picked up the files and began to work on the ads.

A half hour later, after talking to an understanding Maxwell, Jackie headed home. Changing into jeans, an oversized sweatshirt and sneakers, she started to clean for Kathy's visit, picking up the cloths she had stripped off the night before. Stripping the bed, she tried to push the memories of the nights of passion she and Chad had shared out of her mind by busying herself with chores.

Chapter 10

Chad had spent the morning looking for the perfect engagement ring, finding a ring that would reflect the love he felt for her. He decided on a prong set diamond with two slightly tapered, channel set banquette diamonds on either side.

He was so excited about giving Jackie the ring he had decided that he would get the ring sized when they returned home. He knew that Jackie would argue about leaving, but after the nights of passion they shared, he knew that she loved him.

He couldn't stop smiling as he made his way to her office, wondering how she would like the ring. Her secretary saw him coming and sat up straighter, fluffing her long brown hair and giving him her full attention.

He was surprised when he asked to see Jackie, only to find out that she wasn't at work.

"Miss Williams took some personal time off, Mr. Simons, but she turned your account over Mr. Webber, would you like to talk to him?"

He knew Jackie and Lawrence were close, and he needed answers. Maybe Lawrence had them. He would do anything to figure out what was going on with her.

The secretary led him to the office where Lawrence stood to greet him. He thought the man looked a bit uncomfortable, did he know something? Chad looked around the office, noticing the African artwork that was similar to the art in Jackie's office. His eyes grew wide in surprise when he saw a painting of Jackie.

Lawrence did not miss the reaction Chad had when his eyes landed on the painting.

"You like it? I did that a year ago, when we went to Florida together."

Chad did like the picture. In the painting she was on a beach, her long black hair blowing wildly in the wind. She wore only a blue cloth draped loosely around her body. The picture was so beautiful it looked like she could stepped out of the painting. He could see she exposed a very expressive and personal side of herself in the painting. Jealousy reared it's ugly head.

Turning to Lawrence, his blue eyes ice cold, he asked, "Is there something going on between the two of you? Are you in love with her?"

Lawrence seemed amused by the question. "Of course I love her."

He held up his hand to stop an angry Chad from attacking him. "I love her as a dear friend, and she's like my kid sister. Nothing but a great friendship."

Chad could see that he was being honest about his love for Jackie. He flopped heavily into a leather chair, his jaw ticking.

Lawrence sat down in a chair opposite him. "Listen, Jackie has always been a good friend, she has always been there to support me. Now I'll admit that when I first met her I wanted something more than friendship, but I believe from the first day I met her, and up until now, she's been hung up on you."

Sarcastically, Chad replied, "So hung up on me she fights me tooth and nail every time I try bring us together? How much can I do before I should just give up?"

Lawrence sat thinking, and chose his words carefully. "Have you ever thought because of her mother leaving, and her father drinking himself to death, she's afraid she could end up heartbroken, like her father?"

Chad slumped back in his chair. "God, I've been wanting a life with her for so long. What do I have to do get her to see that?"

Lawrence shrugged, wishing he could be more help. "That I can't tell you, but I hope you can make it work."

***

Jackie folded the last plastic bag, putting away the last of the food she had purchased for Kathy's visit. She looked around. Nothing left to do but wait for Chad.

As if on cue, the door bell rang.

Standing in the doorway, dressed causal in jeans and a black form-fitting t-shirt with a black leather jacket, he looked so good it was hard for Jackie to keep her mind on giving him the news about Kathy, and not drag him in the bedroom.

Smiling, he walked in and lifted her up, kissed her, and kicked the door closed with his foot. He put her back on the floor. "I went by your office. You taking time off? What, you want to spend all day and night making love?"

She looked up at him and shook her head. "Kat called. She's coming to stay with me for awhile."

Taking her hand, he lead to the small den, sat down in her overstuffed couch and pulled her down onto his lap.

"What's wrong? What's going on with Kathy?"

She leaned back, enjoying his warm embrace.

"She stopped seeing Robert. Her family didn't approve of him. Robert wants to talk to her, and right now she doesn't want to deal with it. She asked to come here, to just to get away for while."

Sighing and shaking his head, he said, "Well, running isn't the answer for her, or for you, Jackie."

Scooting off his lap, she glared at him. "She's not running, and neither am I. She wants space, what's wrong with that?"

His temper was beginning to simmer. "The hell you aren't running! I, for one, have had it!"

He was off the couch and towering over her, but she was not going to let him bully her anymore.

Poking her finger in his hard chest, she yelled, "Maybe if you stop bullying, and just caring about what the hell *you* want, you would know I'm not going to just jump up and give up my life. If you want someone to fall at your damn feet and do what you want, someone to do your bidding, then you need to get Misty!"

He grabbed her arms, gritting his teeth. "Is that what you want? Fine! Maybe you're right! Maybe I should have been with Misty all this time, instead of chasing after you, because it's obvious you don't want to be with me. Hell, at least Misty knows what she wants, *she's* not running hot and cold all the damn time."

Letting her arms go, he reached into his pocket, took out a small box, and slapped it in her hand. Storming out of the room, he didn't look back, afraid if he did, he would fall apart.

Jackie jumped as the heavy oak door slammed so hard it shook the pictures on the walls. Sinking down on the couch, she opened the box. Tears spilled down her face at the sight of what was inside.

Taking the ring out of the box she slid it on her finger, a perfect fit.

She knew because of her fear of being hurt that she had pushed the only man she loved away. She sat in the lonely silence, hoping that she could get over what she knew was lost to her.

Chapter 11

Chad sat in his car, in the long-term parking at the airport, thinking. None of his plans had worked. He had hoped to bring Jackie with him, but instead all he got was a promise from Lawrence to forward his finished ads to him for his approval and that he would be there for Jackie.

Even though the hour was late, he didn't want to go home. He decided to go to Robert's apartment and check on him. He wondered if Robert had bounced back from his break up with Kathy. He wished he could be more like Robert. Robert never allowed women to affect him, not the way he had let Jackie get to *him*.

Upon arriving, Chad was shocked at his friend's appearance. Robert had always been well-groomed and put together. He always took pride in himself and his good looks, but now he was a mess. No, he looked like hell. Rumpled clothing that looked like he hadn't changed in days, his usually neatly cut hair was longer and uncombed and plastered to his head and he was unshaven as well.

"Chad, what's up, my man?" Robert mumbled as he walked back into the living room and flopping down on the leather sofa.

Chad followed, still shocked at seeing his friend in such a state. "Well, I should be asking you that. Robert, you look a mess, buddy."

Robert chuckled, running a hand over his bearded face. He knew that he was a sorry sight. "Let's see. The woman that I fell hopelessly in love with told me she doesn't want to see me ever again. Hell, I never saw it coming. Falling for her, I mean. You know, us falling in love and everything, at the time we were just trying to get you and Jackie together, and before I knew what happened, BLAM! Yeah, I'm a mess alright."

Getting up, Robert went into his small kitchen and brought back two bottles of beer, handed one to Chad, and took his seat again.

"How did things go with Jackie? I can only guess, not good, since you're here with me."

Looking at Robert, he gave him a hurt and defeated look. "I didn't do any better than you. I don't know about you, but part of me wants to say to hell with it, but I just can't."

Robert held his beer in the air for a toast. "Here's to patience, we'll need it."

***

Finishing the last of the "Death by Chocolate" ice cream cake, Jackie and Kathy sat watching their tenth tearjerker movie. After all, what would a two-week pity party be without a sad movie?

Kathy looked at the empty cake plate, wiping her eyes. "Girl, this feeling sorry for ourselves is going to make us both fat."

Jackie nodded as she rubbed her belly, then grabbed her phone. "Yeah, we may as well go all the way. How about pizza and hot wings?"

Another sad movie, twenty-four wings and a large supreme pizza later, Kathy made another observation. "You know we look like crap, don't you?"

Kathy pulled her sweatshirt over her knees and tossed the remote to Jackie. Her mind couldn't stay off Robert. She wanted to know how he was, and if he was with someone else. The very thought made her to feel sick to her stomach. She turned to Jackie with a defeated sigh. "Yeah, I feel about as bad as I look. I don't know about you, but I know I made a terrible mistake."

Jackie nodded in agreement as she bit into the last chicken wing, tossing the bone on her plate. She licked the hot sauce from her fingers.

"Well, what are we going to do about it?" Kathy asked, frustrated at the whole mess that she had put herself in. And all because she had listened to her mother and brother, and not her heart. Thinking, Jackie picked up the last slice of pizza and tore it in half, handing one piece to Kathy.

She bit into the pizza and slowly chewed as a plan formed. A slow smile crept across her face. "It depends on how willing you are to make things right with them, Kathy."

Looking at her friend's eager face, she already knew the answer. Kathy was more than willing to do anything to get her man back.

Jumping up from the couch, she tossed the remaining pizza bit back into the greasy pizza box and excitedly pulled Kathy up, then proceeded to pull her down the hall to her bedroom.

"Come on, we need to do some planning,"

Kathy couldn't help but notice the twinkle had returned to her friend's brown eyes. She could only guess what Jackie was planning to do to get Chad back.

Chapter 12

"Son, you need to pull yourself together. No woman is worth all this," David Buckland told Robert, who was slouching on his couch, mooning over a woman like a lovesick teenager.

"I need you at the mill. The paperwork and orders are getting backlogged. You're the one who runs the mill. Hell, I'm too old to be there all the time, we need you back."

David shook his head. He knew his pleas were falling on deaf ears. He had never seen his son this way. It had been two weeks and his boy hadn't came into work, hadn't called, or even answered his phone. *He fell really hard for this girl,* David thought as he looked at his son.

The way Robert was acting was really beginning to worry him. He should have seen this coming. Kathy had been the only woman he dated more than a few times, or even bothered to talk about.

At that moment David called himself every kind of fool. He

had pressured his son to leave the young woman alone, and he regretted the words he had spoken to Kathy. Robert sighed he did not care about working or any advice his father may have to offer. "Dad, I'll be back to work on Monday, or Wednesday. Stop worrying."

David gave one more try to lift his sons spirits. "Look here, son, why don't you go out? It's Saturday. You know several young ladies who would love it if you gave them a call. Several of them have been calling the mill since they heard you were, uhmmm, free again. You might enjoy going out with someone who can get your mind off your troubles."

Robert looked at his dad, astounded by his comment. He shook his head, trying his best not to get angry with his father. "No, Dad, I don't want to go out, and I don't want to spend time with just any woman. I don't know how many times I have to say this...I love Kathy."

Not wanting to hear anymore of his father's unwanted advice Robert got up and walked into his bathroom to take a much needed shower.

Not feeling very hospitable to his father, he called out to him. "Dad, you can let yourself out, I'm gonna grab a shower and go to bed."

David hoped his meddling wouldn't cause permanent damage to his relationship with his son, and Robert wasn't the only one who was unhappy. His own wife wasn't very pleased with him at the moment, either, for not supporting Robert. She had promised David no peace until he set things right with his son, and stay out of Robert and Kathy's relationship.

Hearing the shower running he got up to leave.

Kathy had been standing outside the door, working up the courage to go inside to face Robert. She had thought to ring the doorbell, but decided to use the key Robert gave her. Hands trembling, she put the key in the door, thinking, *Now or never.*

She prayed he didn't have a woman in the apartment, and especially not in his bed. She stood a bit, then put a determined look on her face. If there *was* woman in there, the wench would be leaving. That was one thing she was sure of.

Slowly, she opened the door and came face to face with Robert's father. Groaning, and bracing herself for a fight, she stood tall and looked into to his eyes. She was determined to stand her ground. She was she was astounded at what happened next.

The man engulfed her in a tight embrace, then quickly let her go. "Kathy, it's good to see you! What are you standing out there for? Come on in here, honey!"

Kathy looked as if she half expected someone to yell "Gotcha!"

Here stood Robert's dad, grinning like he was the Joker, saying it was good to see her, and ushering her into his son's apartment! The same man who days earlier wanted her to have nothing to do with his son. Looking dumbfounded, she tried to shake off the shock she felt, and then stammered. "I...I...wanted to speak with Robert in private."

David stood smiling like he was in a toothpaste commercial and ushered her into the living room. "Robert's in the shower. He's going to be so happy to see you! Now, when you get time I want you to come to my house to have dinner with my wife and me. We want to get to know you better."

Having said that, he wanted to give them privacy, so he left, smiling and relieved. He couldn't wait to get home and tell his wife that things were fixed. Kathy watched the man leave, not quite believing what he had just said. Returning to her senses, she heard the shower going, and smiled. She tossed her bag and keys on the coffee table and made her way to Robert's bathroom. She undressed, letting the clothing fall to the floor.

Robert stood in the shower letting the hot water beat against his skin. Although the water was steaming, hot his body and mind were numb to it. His eyes closed tightly, his mind brought forth images of Kathy. He could see her laughing at him when she tried to teach him the latest dance step. He loved how the little dimple popped out on her right cheek, and how those lovely brown eyes seem to light up like a Christmas tree. Oh! How he missed her!

How could she have such a strong hold on him! She had somehow gained possession of his heart in such a short amount of time. Truth be told, he fell for her the day at the swimming hole. She was the woman of his dreams—beautiful, didn't take crap from anyone, intelligent, and light-hearted.

If she didn't come back and let him try to convince her to see him, it would kill him.

He would move on, what other choice was there, but he knew he would never love another woman like this.

"Jesus, I'm acting like we've been together for years, but we've only been together weeks. This is insane."

A soft voice jolted him from his daydream. "Mind if I join you?"

Recognizing the whisper that came from outside the shower door, his heart leapt in his throat. Opening his eyes, he quickly closed them when soap suds got in his eyes. He cursed and splashed hot water in his face. Opening his eyes again, he blinked a few times as if he could not believe that she was really standing before him.

She was smiling as she pulled the door open and stood waiting for his response to her request. His eyes slowly roved over her dark nude body. He had thought he would never see her like that again. She was the most beautiful creature in the world. Nothing could tempt him like she could, and as if his body agreed with him. his manhood raged to life. Taking her hand, he pulled her into the shower. He pulled her into an almost painful embrace, closed his eyes, and kissed her brow.

Relieved at his reaction, Kathy rested her head on his hard chest and wrapped her arms around his trim waist.

"Does this mean you want to be with me?" Robert asked hopefully.

Giggling like a little girl, she raised up on her toes and kissed him softly on his lips, then released a pleased sigh. "Hmmmm…Yes, it does."

Pushing her back against the shower wall, he kissed her so passionately it was making her squirm. He wanted nothing more than to make love to her, worship her body, and tell her how much he truly was crushed by her leaving.

But they had to come to an understanding before they could move forward. "What about your brother and my father?"

He could see a brief look of sadness cross her face, but then she smiled and nodded.

Kathy had gone to see her family before she came to see Robert, and things had gotten heated after she told them that he had every intention of having a relationship with Robert. Her brother left the house, saying that he would not speak to his sister again until she left Robert alone.

Her mother gave in a little, saying that she wouldn't accept Robert, but she was an adult and her daughter, and she would love her and always want to be in her life. She smiled up at the man that held her heart in his strong hands, wrapping her legs around his waist, she gave him a toe tingling kiss.

"What about them? They'll just have to deal with it. Baby, I want you, that's all that matters to me right now. I love you."

Her words brought the fire back into his soul. His head felt light as he felt her grind her body against his throbbing manhood. She slowly allowed him to slide into her. He wanted her so bad all thoughts were quickly fluttering away from his mind. Grinding his teeth he held back for one moment.

"Kat, when things get rough you're not going to bolt on me again, are you?"

She felt a pang in her heart, and tears gathered in her eyes. She gently touched his face. He looked tired and uncertain, she could see the hurt in his eyes. She knew she had caused his pain by not staying by his side.

"I'll never leave you again. I let other people define what our relationship was about instead of asking you straight out what you wanted from me. That won't happen again."

Gasping as he thrust into her warm passage, he put all his love into every thrust and every caress.

He whispered, "For the record, what I want is you in my life as my one and only lady. I love you. All I ask is for you to let me love you."

He kissed her with such hunger she felt like she was going to pass out. When they broke the wild kiss they were both panting. Groans of pleasure echoed in the bathroom. Both of them reached their euphoric release at the same time. Laying her head on his shoulder, she was totally spent, and happier than she had been in two weeks.

"I love you, too, Robert. I felt awful when I was away from you."

Holding onto her he turned the shower off and stepped out, dragging her with him. She giggled and tried to get him to let her go so she could dry herself.

"You can let me go now, Robert."

He grabbed the thick towel from his bathroom sink and began drying her off. "Oh no, you're not getting out of my sight, woman. The last time I did that, it was two weeks of pure hell!"

He shook his head and gave her a playful look, but quickly became serious again. "Kathy, I know some folks, like my father and your brother, would say it's too soon. Hell, they would say this is foolish. But, baby, I know what I want, and I want to marry you."

He rushed his words, hardly believing that he was saying them himself.

He placed his finger on her full lips to stop her from speaking, he felt he had to say everything he had to say now.

"We don't have to rush it. We can go tomorrow and pick out a ring to your liking, and when you're ready you can put it on. Only when *you* are ready will we tell everyone our plans, but please say that you will marry me. Please, make me whole, darling."

He held his breath as he watched the emotions play on her face, and he released a breath when her face lit up. She smiled and nodded, blinking back tears of happiness.

Now it was her time to give him his little surprise. "I'm glad you feel that way, because the tickets I brought would be a waste otherwise."

Robert gave her a curious look. He knew she was up to something, her dark eyes held a secret.

She couldn't hold back any longer, and broke out in joyous laughter. She cupped Robert's face and kissed him tenderly. "I thought we would take a trip to Vegas!" she said, as he swept her up and carried her into his bedroom.

Robert couldn't be happier about the little announcement. He let out a loud whoop, and fell on the bed with her.

"Looks like Dad will be taking care of the mill for another week or two."

He gently kissed her and caressed her smooth skin. He was

so thankful that he had a second chance with the woman who would always possess his soul.

***

Jackie glanced at the engagement ring on her hand. It seemed so natural. She took a deep breath. She didn't know what she would do if Chad had moved on, but she had no one to blame but herself.

Entering Simmons Furniture's corporate office, she was directed to Chad's office on the third floor.

Stepping off the elevator she was surprised to see Linda Owen sitting behind the desk, and even more surprised to find out that she was Chad's aide.

Linda smiled brightly when she spotted her. "Jackie, how are you doing?" the woman asked as she stepped around the desk and engulfed Jackie in a warm embrace.

The open friendliness surprised Jackie, but she hugged the woman back. "I'm fine, Linda. It's good to see you again. I was wondering if I could see Chad, if he's not too busy."

Linda was more than happy to let him know that she wanted to see him. She picked up the phone and buzzed him. "Jackie is here to see you."

She couldn't hide her excitement, maybe Jackie coming to him would actually help Chad's mood. He was a good boss, but since returning from his trip he had been a bit difficult to deal with. He would get upset over the simplest things, then would spend hours closed up in his office, not talking to anyone except her.

Earlier in the day Misty had come around, hoping that she could have another shot at Chad. The foolish woman had stormed past Linda and gone into Chad's office. The first words out her mouth were how foolish he had been chasing after Jackie, and now he should come to his senses.

Needless to say, Chad told her in a very colorful way to never get in his face again, and to leave his damned office before he had her arrested for trespassing.

Linda smiled, knowing Jackie being here would give Chad the peace and happiness he wanted. So, naturally, she was stunned when he responded to her angrily.

"Tell her I'm busy, and she should do like everyone else who wants to see me. Make a damned appointment."

The smile fell from Linda's face as she hung up the phone and stammered. " I...I'm sorry. He said he was busy at the moment and that you need to make an appointment."

Jackie was a bit surprised and hurt by Chad's refusal. She tried to mask her hurt. After all, it was a very real possibility that he would not want to see her and she was going have to accept it.

Clearing her throat she started to back away, wanting to leave before she started crying and made an even bigger fool of herself.

"Oh...yeah...alright...thank you, Linda...goodbye, take care." Her shoulders slumped, she turned to leave with her pride shattered and her heart broken.

Linda let out an exasperated breath and rolled her eyes to the heavens at the foolishness she was witnessing. Taking matters into her own hands, she marched to Jackie, turned her around, and grabbed her arm. She dragged her to the office door and grumbled to her. "At this rate, you two will get together when you're both sixty. I swear, my two-year-old acts more grown up than you two. I can't believe that two smart and successful people are acting so silly and immature. You both need to grow the hell up, and if you want to be together, do it!"

Finished with her rant, Linda yanked Chad's office door open and pushed Jackie inside. For added effect, she slammed the door, hard.

She stood looking at him, her brown eyes were big and looked like a deer caught in the headlights. She braced herself for the worst.

"Where's Linda? How the hell did you get in here? I told her I was busy."

Jackie turned to leave the room before he got angrier than he already was. Her hand was on the handle when Chad's angry grimace turned to panic and sorrow, sorrow he had treated her so hatefully. His heart was beating so fast he feared he would have a heart attack.

Jumping up so fast his chair slammed against the wall, he called to her, his voice a little louder than he meant it to be.

"Jackie! Wait...stop, don't open the door."

Almost afraid to see anger on his face she hesitated before turning around. She stood looking at him, seemingly drained of all emotion.

"Why are you here, Jackie?" His blue eyes stayed trained on her, his voice was soft, but his features were stony and unreadable. With steady strides he went to her. Stopping inches in front of her, he was so close she had to tip her head back to look him in the eyes.

"I'm here...to say I'm sorry about the things I said to you." Her voice was barely a whisper.

Shifting from one foot to the other, she had hoped this would be easier, but looking at the stern look on his face she knew he was not going to let her off easy.

Chad had to ball his fists at his sides to keep from grabbing her and hugging the hell out of her, but he didn't. Instead, he took a deep breath. Narrowing his eyes a bit, as if he was trying to look into her soul, he spoke again. "Is that it? Is that all you have to say to me, sunshine?"

She couldn't fight the urge to touch his face. Gently laying her hand on his handsome face, she knew Linda was right, it was time to grow up, and she was going to say what she had to say.

"No. that's not all."

She closed her eyes and took a deep breath. "I love you, and if you want me, I would be so honored if you would be my husband."

She thought at first he would refuse because he hesitated. Then a slow grin began to spread. But instead of answering her, he went to his desk and picked up the phone.

Looking at Jackie, he spoke. He said, "Linda, hold all my calls, please. And while you're at it, cancel all my evening appointments."

He laughed at Linda's response, and hung the phone up.

Jackie felt her knees go weak when he gave her a sexy lopsided grin and walked towards her like a big game cat, stalking his prey.

"Linda says she'll make sure no one bothers us, as long as we keep the noise to a dull roar."

Jackie could feel her face burning with embarrassment.

Gently, he pulled her into his strong arms. His hand crept up her dark thigh moving her skirt up around her hips. He walked her towards the office door, pinning her between his big body and it. He lifted her up and his fingers hooked her lacy panties and pulled them slowly down.

She moaned as his calloused hand caressed her most intimate spots.

He nipped her ear and whispered to her, "Shhhhh, we wouldn't want anyone to know I'm taking liberties with the soon-to-be Mrs. Simmons."

Epilogue

Ten months later, Jackie stood looking at herself in the full-length mirror, running her hands down her dress. It clung alluringly to her every curve. Smiling, she pushed a fat curl off her shoulder, and her smile wavered a bit.

The day was perfect, but she wished that her father could be with her, to share her happiness, and be the one to walk her down the aisle.

She shook the sad thought off and turned to see Kathy and Linda arranging the train of her gown.

"I'm glad I got married in Vegas, this would make me crazy. Not to mentioning Robert. The boy almost passed out while we were getting married in The Chapel of Love."

Jackie laughed. Her friend and her new husband had picked one of the cheesiest wedding chapels on the Vegas strip. The preacher was dressed like Elvis, right down to the big sunglasses and big belly. The organist was a Mae West impersonator. And

Mae was chomping on a cigar. It also didn't help matters that she and Robert were tipsy from the complimentary champagne the hotel put in the bridal suite.

Poor Robert was swaying, and interrupted the preacher, proclaiming his undying love for Kathy, while Kathy giggled during the ceremony. She came back to the present and waddled around Jackie, checking her hair to make sure the thick curls were in place before she helped her put on the veil. Kathy was eight months pregnant with twins, she could not have been happier. Robert was so proud that he showed the sonogram to anyone and everyone who cared to look.

Touching her swollen belly, she felt one of the twins dancing on her bladder.

"Well, let's get this show on the road, girl."

Putting the veil on Jackie's head, she led her friend to the door, where Lawrence was there waiting to walk her down the aisle, taking the place of her father.

Lawrence was a loyal friend, and had been honored when she asked him to walk with her in her father's stead. He had even gotten her a gift for her wedding day—a locket with a small painting he did of her father.

"Wow, Jackie, you look beautiful. I have to take a picture so I can paint it later, to capture what a breathtaking bride you are."

As the wedding march started, the church full of friends and well wishers stood, watching the bride make her entrance. Jackie could see no one else but the handsome man who would, moments from now, be her friend, her lover, her companion, her *husband*, for life.

Not the end…just the beginning

Printed in the United States
70343LV00002B/55

9 781424 103867